Excerpt from Love's Touch-Then and Now

The tall, brown-haired man with blue eyes looked so very familiar. She backed up a step as he slid the glass door open. She began to feel every joint in her body turn to mush.

"Connor?" she whispered.

The man looked at her and stopped in his tracks. He stared at her for a moment and smiled slightly. "Lizzie?" he said, loud enough for her to hear, then he took a step toward her.

Kate took a step sideways and got tangled with her cane. She fell over and landed hard on her arm and hip. He squatted down beside her, and asked if she was okay. "How is this possible?" she whispered, again.

"Where have you been?" He put out his hand.

Lauren Marie

LOVE'S TOUCH
Then and Now

Lauren Marie

DEDICATION

This one is dedicated to my surrogate family, Jan, Steve and Jacob Schafer. I thank you for your love, support, patience, and all the other adjectives in the dictionary for thirty-six odd years of friendship. Here's to thirty-six more...ack, cough, sputter.

ACKNOWLEDGEMENTS:

Thanks go to Jennifer Conner and the folks at Books to Go, Now, for the opportunity, editing, and art-work. It's so great to be working with you.

I'm still thanking my cousin, Chip Davis, for his incredible support. Mannheim Steamroller rocks. www.mannheimsteamroller.com.

Thank you to my friends and family for their love and support, too.

Thanks, as always, to my readers, Elizabeth Ainsley (you're still hired) and Cindy Simonson (about those roses). Your feed back has been great and helpful. Caitlin Rettinghouse (SOA unite) congrats on the new baby girl. Tiffany Wilde-Hinnenkamp, I know we'll meet again.

This story was started on a manual typewriter in the 1980's after I'd had a dream. No, really, I had a dream that gave me the idea. It later was transferred to an IBM personnel computer that took up the top of my six foot desk. In 1995 I transferred it to a Compaq that actually had spell-check. In the early 2000's it went to my new Dell PC and three years ago, you guessed it, I transferred it again. When I started the story, people didn't have cell phones, lap-tops or DVD players. I had to upgrade it a lot. I hope you enjoy.

Lauren Marie

Prologue - Wedding Day

Lizzie saw the flames dance around her and felt their heat.

When she regained her wits, she found herself lying on top of her husband, who'd landed at an odd angle. She tried to get up, but found it difficult to move. She looked down at his blue eyes, and saw they stared straight up. He was dead. She put her hand over his eyes to close the lids and rested her head back down on his chest and waited.

***

The sky was so blue and the clouds rolled in the light breeze. She felt her husband's hand on her waist as he directed her around the dance floor. It was their first waltz as a married couple. She was nervous at first, but Connor kept them moving around the dance floor with grace. Her heart settled into a calmer rhythm.

Connor kissed her and she smiled. His hand held hers tight and she could feel the warmth from his fingers. This was her day and she wanted to remember every moment. She could still hear the reverend's voice when he'd said the words which they repeated after him - to love, honor and cherish. He'd blessed them, said a prayer, and then they kissed.

They'd kissed before, but this one was special. This kiss she would always remember. She smiled at Connor and gazed into his blue eyes.

When the band finished playing the song they danced to, her father came over to them and her new husband passed her hand onto his father-in-law. Connor then walked across the room to his new mother-in-law and escorted her out onto the makeshift floor. When the band began another dance number other couples came out to waltz.

She saw Connor glance over her mother's shoulder and follow her with his eyes. She wore all lace and satin and her hair was piled on top of her head. She couldn't wait for him to pull it down. He preferred her hair down and loose.

After the dance, Lizzie made her way down the stairs on Connor's arm to the park next to the church, where they received congratulations from family and friends and then the party began. It was a bright and warm day for June.

She could hear laughter and music. The ladies in town outdid themselves with the food and her mother made a wonderful wedding cake. The tables were covered with trays of fresh meats, salads, vegetables and pickles. The ladies from her church group produced a multitude of pickles. She wondered briefly if they were from last year's canning. It felt too early in the season for pickles. *What a day to think about pickles*, she thought and laughed at herself. She spoke with one of the older women about canning, but later couldn't remember what was said. Some of the boys from the stockyards brought moonshine and things got a little livelier. When someone told her that the punch was spiked, she only laughed and did not want to worry. They cut the two-tiered cake and exchanged bites.

While they cut the cake to share with their guests, she saw her sisters. Two of them smiled broadly, but the one sister - two years younger than she - smirked. She'd been jealous of her from the very first moment it became obvious Connor only had eyes for Lizzie. The sister had a terrible crush on him, but Lizzie just smiled back at them. Today was her day and she wouldn't let her sister make her feel guilty.

She couldn't help thinking about later that night after the party when all the guests were gone and they'd be alone. The night before, her mother talked with her about relations between men and women on their wedding night and explained in some detail what would be expected of her. Lizzie and Connor already made love once.

During their courtship over the last several months, they'd fought the excitement they felt for one another. For Lizzie the desire and heat felt overwhelming. Three nights ago, they'd gone for a walk after dinner. They'd gone further out than their usual evening strolls, and followed paths through a grove of fruit trees and came together for the first time in an old, deserted barn. She joked about the snake in the garden, but still wrapped her legs around his waist.

This afternoon, Connor looked across the dance floor and smiled at her. Her father kissed her hand and led her back to her groom. He then took her mother's hand and danced again.

The white, soft clouds flew over their heads and the day went by like a dream. She felt amazed at how quickly the party ended and they prepared to leave.

A carriage with two bay horses, decorated with roses and sweet peas, pulled up in front of the church. Connor helped her climb abroad, then joined her and they waved to their family and friends gathered around. She threw her bouquet to the single ladies and the carriage began to move away. They rode silently most of the way across town to the Broadview Hotel. Her father rented a suite for them for two days and nights.

The room was quietly decorated with bouquets of sweet fragrance flowers. It was heavenly, but she didn't see much of it. She felt very nervous. Now that she was his wife, she thought she needed to prove herself.

Connor took off his jacket and walked toward her. Taking her hand, he kissed the back of it and, as if he'd read her mind, said, "You have nothing to be afraid of, my lass. We'll need to teach each other and that will take time. It's not a thing you can teach or learn in that school of yours." He smiled again and she laughed. Then he put his hands on her hips and placed his lips on hers. Her tension evaporated and she felt nothing but joy.

They laughed as he stumbled while he took off his pants, and laughed again when she couldn't get the laces on her shoes untied. They found reasons to laugh off and on as their motion stuttered, and then grew quietly serious again as the movement became more fluid. They didn't leave each other's arms once, but held on tight at first, and then more gently. Finally, they lay on top of the sheets. Lizzie rested her hand on Connor's chest and felt his hair and sweat. It was a long day and they were both very tired.

Sometime later, she awoke to see smoke blow in the window of their suite. She shook Connor awake and said, "Fire!" He put on his slacks and told her to put on her dressing gown quickly. She could see the haze of smoke in the room as he lit the oil-burning lamp. When he opened the door to the room, she could hear people shouting downstairs.

When Connor put out his hand, she took it and followed him into the hallway where the smoke became very thick and she found it difficult to breathe. She could see the stairwell on fire, but as far as she knew it was the only way down.

He moved Lizzie back into the room, and they went to the window to look outside. The wooden overhang beneath the window blazed with fire and she saw people run with water in buckets from the well across the street, then throw it on the flames. Connor said they would have to try the stairs and guided her back to the passage.

When they reached the top of the stairwell, she could see a small path that ran down the middle of the risers. They hurried, but half-way down, the stair crumbled beneath them. Connor wrapped his arm around her waist as they started to descend. Midway down Lizzie heard something crack and felt as though she were flying.

Chapter One

When she woke up, she tried to catch her breath. Her throat felt dry and sore, and she couldn't swallow. She heard someone's voice say she was delirious which could be caused by the painkillers.

All she could see were Connor's dead eyes as he gazed up at her. Somehow, someone saved her from the fire. Her mind spun and she went into a black place. She wanted to scream out in grief over his death, but she couldn't form words. The sadness choked her and she wanted to shriek at God for taking him.

She slowly peeled her eyelids off her eyes and saw a nondescript, gray ceiling. A strange sound beeped in her ear somewhere above her head and it annoyed her to no end. She tried to clear her throat, but it felt so dry, all she could do was gasp.

She saw a woman look down at her and realized it was her mother's face. The woman smiled. How could her mother smile when Connor was dead?

"Hey sweetheart, welcome back."

"He's dead, mother," she whispered and started to cough and cry at the same time.

"Henry's not dead. In fact, he doesn't have a scratch on him. He bumped his head on the windshield, but he's fine. He doesn't have a concussion or brain damage either, thank God. Your car will need a lot of work, but at least you weren't killed. We'll have to talk about that car. I think you may need to get a new one," her mother said.

"Who's Henry?" she asked.

"Kate, he's your boyfriend. You do remember him, don't you? Maybe you bumped your head, too and have a little amnesia."

"I'm so thirsty," Kate said and slipped back into sleep. What did her mother mean, a car? Connor died at the hotel.

Later, she opened her eyes again and could see a little more clearly. Her mom sat beside the bed and read the newspaper.

The older woman looked up and smiled. "There you are, Kate." She got up from the chair, helped Kate adjust the pillows behind her head and move the back of the bed up. She left the room and soon reappeared with Kate's dad. He walked around the bed, leaned on the other side and took her hand.

She tried to speak, but she had no strength in her voice and found it difficult to get the words out. She tried to sit up, but felt stiff from the neck down and her legs felt heavy. She could only whisper, "Where am I?"

"You're in the hospital, honey. Do you remember anything?" her dad asked.

Her mom handed her a cup with ice chips, and a spoon and Kate scooped some into her mouth. It helped with the dryness and after a few more spoonfuls she cleared her throat. "I remember there was a fire and that Connor died. We fell through the stairs at the hotel." Tears rolled down Kate's cheeks.

"No sweetheart, your beat up, old VW got wrapped around a tree. The steering wheel hit you in the stomach and the paramedics think you jammed your foot into the floor when you tried to use the brake to stop the car. You dislocated your hip. A very skilled orthopedic doctor operated on you and put some screws in there to hold your hip together. I wish you'd sell that car," her mom added.

Her father squeezed her hand and said that Henry was fine. Kate closed her eyes and tried to understand what they said. Her brain went in fifteen different directions at once and all she really wanted to do was go back to sleep, but she needed to get grounded again. She needed to understand what happened. Then she remembered the dreams.

She'd always had strange ones. They seemed to take place in a different time and world, and she always felt fine afterward. But this was the first time anyone died. It bothered her, but one thing bothered her more - she remembered the accident.

"Mom, I wasn't driving. Henry drove after the party," she said. The name Henry made no sense to her. It was Connor she remembered. She glanced around the room and heard the beeping noise again. She looked above her head, and saw a heart monitor and an IV pole and then it all slammed back into her mind. She realized that both of the people she'd dreamt about all her life, died in a fire. She felt empty and sad.

"Oh, I must have misunderstood him. I thought he said you were driving," her mom said.

She saw her parents exchange glances. She saw that the worry lines around her father's eyes had gotten deeper.

"I wasn't driving, dad."

"That's weird. Henry said the paramedics told him that you tried to put your foot through the floor of the car," her dad said and frowned. "Are you having any pain? It is almost time for a shot? The nurse said you could have it a little earlier if it helps."

"Not yet. I'm okay. I just feel groggy." She brought her hand up and rubbed her eyes. "This is just too weird, the crash..." her voice faded.

"You don't remember?" her father asked.

"I remember a fire. I can still smell the smoke. Maybe it was the dream," Kate whispered.

"Not that again," her mom said. Kate's father started to say something from across the bed, but she interrupted him. "I thought you stopped having those years ago after you saw that counselor."

"Not now, Maggie." Kate's father looked at his daughter and kissed her hand. "You just woke up. We can go over it later. I'll go see about another shot and call Henry to let him know you're awake."

Her mom took her other hand and held it tight. "We sent him home to get some rest. It was strange that he didn't stay after the hospital released him, but he came in yesterday and sat with you all night."

Kate held onto her dad's hand. "No Dad. I don't need a shot yet. I'm just trying to remember."

"I know, baby. Don't worry about that right now," he said and squeezed her hand.

"Daddy, they died. I saw them die in the fire," she said and felt her throat tighten.

Her dad looked across the bed at her mom. "Maggie, did you tell her about that?"

"No, Ian, I didn't say a thing. She must have been awake during the accident."

"Sweetheart, those boys driving the SUV had a higher blood alcohol level than you or Henry. They crossed into your lane," her father said. "I'm not real happy with you or Henry for drinking and driving, but we can discuss that later."

Kate looked at both her parents, unable to comprehend what they said. She tried to work it out. "Do you mean the boys that hit us died?"

"Isn't that who you were talking about, Kate?" her mom snapped.

"Sure," she answered and looked up. "That's what I meant." She saw her father's frown deepen.

15

Lauren Marie

Her mom shook her head. "I'm going to find some coffee. Do you want a cup, Ian?"

When she left the room, Kate watched him turn back to her and cross his arms. "So, tell me. What did you see?"

"The man and woman I've been seeing in my dreams all these years, got married," she said. As quickly as she could she told him about what she'd witnessed. Her mom never could understand her dreams. Kate wasn't sure she understood them either.

After a few minutes, her mom came back into the room with two cups of coffee. She handed one to her husband.

"Mom, did Henry really say I was driving?" Kate asked.

"As I said, sweetheart, I must have misunderstood him," Maggie answered, and sipped her coffee.

"Who were the people, killed in the other car?" She looked at both her parents.

"Kate, that's not important right now," her dad said and kissed her hand, again. "You've got some recovering to do. That should be your focus."

"Was something else broken besides my hip?" she asked. Exhaustion took over her brain and she found it hard to focus her thoughts.

"No, and it wasn't broken. Your hip was dislocated when you pushed your foot down on the floor of the car. They thought you might have a skull fracture, but it was only a concussion. The x-ray's were normal," her mom said. "Too hard-headed I think."

"Thanks Mom." Kate put her head down on the pillow.

"Are you tired sweetheart?" her dad asked.

"Yeah, I'm just going to close my eyes for a minute," she said and fell back to sleep.

Chapter Two

"You can do it; you know you can do it."

"Shut up, Jerry or I'll put my cane down your throat," Kate said between breaths.

"See you've got gumption in there. I can hear it in your voice." He laughed.

Jerry was Kate's physical therapist. He'd worked with her for a week and acted like he knew her every thought. It made her mad. She fought as hard as she could to get her mobility back in shape. Jerry had her on steps today, which she found difficult. She didn't want to stay any longer in the hospital than need be.

"You'll be running a mile again before you know it. Now, just a couple more steps and we'll take a break," he said.

"I like the break idea. Let's see." Kate took a step. She pushed her light brown hair behind her ear and turned around. She slowly took one step down and then the next. "How about I break your hip?"

"Attitude, Kate, that's some attitude. Here, I'm only trying to help you." He moved the wheelchair behind her. "Take it slow sitting back down. No flopping like yesterday."

She slowly lowered herself into the chair and let out a long breath. Sweat trickled down the side of her face. She looked up at Jerry. "This gets easier, right?"

"Right."

Kate needed to get the strength back into her legs. All of the assistants and techs said she was lucky she hadn't needed a hip replacement. She preferred the idea of keeping her own bones. She could only hope. They were a little angry with her since she started to refuse the painkillers. They made her sick to her stomach. If there was one thing she hated worse than going to the dentist, that was being nauseated and throwing up.

Henry only came by to visit her once or twice while she was in the hospital. He claimed to have an aversion to the smell of sick people. Once she moved to the rehabilitation center he showed up more often, but only a little. They hadn't talked much about the accident yet and Kate didn't want to push the subject.

"I've never run a mile."

Jerry patted her on the shoulder. "There's always a first time."

"Just try to keep up with her when she's taking care of patients." They both looked up and saw Kate's dad as he approached them. "You'd think she had roller-skates on her feet." He leaned over and kissed the top of her head. "Hi, sweetie. How's it going today?" He straightened up and shook Jerry's hand.

"Torture, pure torture." She smiled up at Jerry. "But it is getting easier."

"Now that's a first." Jerry laughed, again.

"Are you almost finished for today?" her father asked. "I don't want to interrupt."

"Yeah, we can call it a day. I'll see you bright and ugly tomorrow morning, missy."

"Bright and ugly? Ha, ha, you're so funny. Thanks, Jerry. Have a good day." She took her dad's hand. "So, how come I'm so lucky that my favorite daddy visited me before lunch time?"

"My morning schedule was clear and I thought... hmm...wouldn't it be nice to take my daughter for lunch in the most horrible coffee shop in the hospital?" He smiled down at her.

She laughed. "How can I resist?"

Her dad moved around the back of the chair and began to push her down a long hallway. "Your mother will be by later. She's playing cards or some such thing this afternoon. I'm going to bring Grammy by this evening. She misses you."

"I miss her, too. Tell her to bring jellybeans."

"You're going to rot your teeth out."

"You're not a dentist. I simply must have one bad habit."

He wheeled her through double doors that led to the cafeteria and moved her to a table, took her order and went to retrieve the food. It wasn't that good, but it was nice to be able to spend some time with her dad. She itched to talk to him. After they finished lunch, she folded her napkin on the table and put her hands on the arms of the wheelchair.

"Uh-oh. You've got a serious look on your face." He took a sip of coffee and waited patiently.

Kate started to say something, but stopped and looked at her hands. She didn't know how to start this. "I'm kind of at a loss at how to get going. Dad, I only had one beer at that party and I ate real food."

"What about Henry?" Her dad frowned at her.

"He drank a lot. I should never have gotten into the car with him. I don't know what I was thinking." She put her hands up to her face and rubbed her eyes. "Let's discuss something else."

"What's the subject?" he asked and sat back in his chair.

She took in a deep breath. "Remember all the times we've talked about the dreams I was always having?"

"Yeah." He leaned forward.

"You remember I told you about the couple, Elizabeth and Connor?" He nodded. She closed her eyes and thought, *there's no time like the present.* "When I first woke up, after the accident, I think I had my final dream about them. I dreamt

19

they died. I still can't figure out why I'm so bothered about it. I feel like maybe I should be glad it's over, but all I feel is emptiness. Am I making any sense?"

"So, they died and you haven't had any more dreams about them?" he asked. He shook his head and adjusted in his seat. "It makes sense now. You kept calling out for Connor. I'd forgotten the names. You said it when Henry sat with you. It really annoyed him."

"I'll have to deal with him at some point. We haven't even talked about what happened. The important thing is, in the dream Elizabeth and Connor got married, there was a fire and they died. Dad, I'm not sure what to feel. I know it sounds silly, I mean...oh, I don't know what I mean. When I was a kid it was like story time, but now, is the story over?" She looked at him and silently pled for some answer.

"Sweetheart, I'm afraid this isn't my area of expertise, but I think I know someone who might be able to help. I have a client named Dr. Neil Stein. He is a psychiatrist, but he might know more about dream states than I do. He has an open mind and I'm sure he'll listen."

"Dad, a psychiatrist? I haven't lost my mind," Kate said.

"I know you haven't lost your mind, but you are closing yours to the possibility he might be able to answer some of your questions. Your mother does that, too."

The tone of her dad's voice took Kate by surprise. It also seemed strange that he'd just compared her to her mom. "What do you mean by that?"

"Never mind, just give it a try. I promise he won't make you feel silly. And it would be good for you to discuss your relationship with Henry, too."

"That's already been decided. I was going to break up with him, but the accident happened and I haven't been able to bring it up. He's been so upset about the boys that got killed that night. I didn't want to make him feel worse."

"Kate, you've got to think of yourself now. You're going to be fine in no time, but I don't think Henry will make you happy. That's all I want for you, is to be happy."

"Thanks, Dad. How do you think Mom will take it? She's always thought the world of Henry."

"Your mom may be a little dense sometimes, but right now she's not real pleased with Henry. You know how she likes to be in control of everything and she doesn't think he's going in that direction. He's definitely not in control. It's hard for her to admit, but I don't think she'll fight you on this one, and particularly, since Henry's been cited for DUI and had his license suspended."

Kate took her dad's hand and held it to her cheek. "You're going to make me cry, dad. Henry mentioned the DUI. He's pissed about it. I asked if he thought he could fight it and I didn't get much of an answer. I hope you don't mind if I take a wait and see attitude with Mom?" She squeezed his hand and raised an eyebrow. "Okay, bring on the head shrink. Maybe we'll find out I'm bipolar or something really weird."

He pointed his finger at her. "No joking on that one. It's serious time, okay?"

"Okay."

That afternoon, Dr Neil Stein came to introduce himself and talk with her. Kate liked him the minute he walked in the door. He was tall, with dark hair and a thick mustache and beard. She watched him sit down and he asked her to call him Neil. She felt comfortable and found it easy to talk to him.

She spoke mostly about her relationship with Henry. She explained how she felt and the decisions she'd made before the accident. It was for the best to break up the relationship and she knew it. Neil agreed with her and said it sounded as though she had good judgment.

"There is another subject my dad wants me to talk about," Kate said, and felt calm. "I've been having a recurring dream for, well, all my life." She spent the next half hour describing it and her feelings about it. Neil sat and listened, and never interrupted her. He did correct her once and said it sounded more like a progressive dream rather than recurring.

He said he read some books about how to interpret dreams, but that wasn't his focus in counseling. Fortunately, he did have an open mind and said he could put her in contact with some people he knew would be interested in helping.

After Neil left, she stretched out on her bed and tried to get comfortable enough to take a nap. There was a knock on the door and Henry's blond head appeared. He smiled and carried a bouquet of flowers.

She looked at the man she'd lived with for the last five years and realized she didn't have any strong feelings for him. He was about six foot and wore the California surfer look - blond hair and blue eyes. He kept fit, tanned on a regular basis and looked good, but his drinking had gotten out of hand.

"Hi. I've been waiting for you to finish with that doctor. What's going on?" he asked. He laid the flowers on her stomach and leaned over to give her a kiss.

"There's nothing much going on. We were just talking. It was no biggy." She moved the flowers to the bedside stand.

"That wasn't the doctor that did your surgery. Who was he?" Henry pulled a chair over and sat by the bed.

"He is covering for my doctor, who has the day off. What are you doing here so early?"

"The market's closed for the day and I didn't want to sit around the office anymore. I thought I should come and check on my best girl. I felt I should tell her how much I miss her."

"That's nice. Who's your best girl?" She smiled.

"Ha, ha, very funny, Kate."

They started to discuss superficial things and Kate's mind wandered. She thought about the talk with Neil and hoped he would remember to send her the names of the people who might have answers about the dreams.

The next day she got a message from Neil, with the names Anna and Jeff Sheridan and their phone number. Kate tucked the message into a book and decided to contact them as soon as she was out of the hospital.

Chapter Three

By the end of the third week, Kate wanted to get out of rehab in the worst way. Her parents agreed to let her come back to the family home until she was released to go back to work. She didn't want to go back to the townhouse she and Henry shared.

A few days after she woke up in the hospital, a friend stopped by to visit and said Henry told their friends she was behind the wheel of the car the night the accident happened. He stopped by the same day and Kate chewed on him pretty good. She was furious with him and told him that she'd be at her parents to simmer down. Then he got angry and said he was surprised by her anger. He'd gone silent for a few minutes as though trying to come up with a reasonable explanation, but all he said was that he didn't understand her position, then ended up storming out of the room.

For a few seconds, Kate felt worried she'd stepped over the line with Henry. He'd never done anything to hurt her, but for a moment she thought he might hit her. She should have broken it off a lot sooner. She'd let the relationship go on far too long.

She was filled with guilt. When she got the complete story about the carload of high school kids, who celebrated their football team's win by drinking too much, she decided to wait another couple of weeks before she finalized the breakup. The tragedy was too fresh and she didn't want to throw it back in Henry's face. He did have his license suspended and a DUI on his record.

For some crazy reason Kate would never understand, her mom still believed Henry was the greatest. She couldn't figure out why Kate was so reluctant to commit to him one hundred percent and marry him. In her opinion, Kate needed to assure Henry of her commitment to the relationship and he would settle down and feel more secure. Kate's mom was still in the dark about the fact that the dreams were all she could think about.

The first things she remembered about the dreams were seeing children play. They wore strange clothing and there were ladies in long dresses. There were no cars, but wagons and horses moved up and down dirt roads. She didn't remember her age when she discovered there was no asphalt in the dream - no parking lots or roads with lines.

As the dreams progressed, the children grew up and went to school. In one of the dreams, she walked to the school with two of the girls she always played with and realized, at some point, that they were her younger sisters. They walked past a storefront and she could see her reflection in the window. The little girl who stared back looked like her, but it wasn't her. Kate had light brown hair, but the reflection had blonde curls. She heard someone call, "Lizzie, Lizzie come on. We're going to be late." It was her older sister, Delia. It bothered her when she woke up and thought she was not only going to school awake, but also asleep.

As Kate got older in the dream, she attended dances put on by the local Methodist Church. A young man named Ben Harley, from a well-to-do family, began to pay special attention to her and when she was fifteen he tried to kiss her behind the church. It was a slobbery kiss and she didn't really enjoy it much. She didn't intend to let him try it again.

A year later, Ben said something about marriage and discussed it with her father. When the girl in the dream, Lizzie, started to laugh, he'd looked hurt and didn't mention it again. Lizzie tried to talk to him and explain how much his friendship meant to her, but he just walked away from her. He continued to ingratiate himself with her family and as Lizzie grew older, the more annoying she found his behavior.

While in college, Kate did some research and grew to understand the dreams better. She discovered they were like a story that continued. She never felt afraid of them and discovered that on the nights when she didn't dream, her heart felt empty in the morning.

After she found out that her grandmother had three sisters named Delia, Lizzie and Effie, she tried to get some of the family's history. Her grandmother was the youngest of the four girls.

Kate loved her grandmother very much. After she returned home from college, the older woman called her Lizzie sometimes. She tried to discuss the family with her grandmother, but didn't get very far. The older woman didn't want to discuss her sisters and became angry and si-lent. Kate wondered why it made her grandmother so angry.

***

When Kate's parents took her home from the hospital rehab, her dad explained that her VW was pretty smashed up, but he had a very good mechanic who would have it ready for her by the next week. The shop had a good reputation and her dad was certain they'd make it run better than it did before the accident. Her mom still wanted her to sell it, since she didn't think it was very safe.

As it turned out, Kate felt glad the car would be ready soon. After her mom drove her to physical therapy three times in one week, she said they'd have to make other arrangements - she needed to go to work.

On Wednesday of that week, the auto shop called her dad and said the car would be ready to go on Friday. So that day, he drove Kate to the garage and dropped her at the front door. Her dad told her to call him immediately if there were any problems.

Kate limped into the office with her cane and saw a woman seated behind a counter. Her hair, piled on top of her head, was dyed a vibrant red color. She wore enough make up for three women. The woman looked up as Kate, leaning on her cane, neared the desk.

"Hi, I'm Kate Sullivan. You have my VW ready to be picked up," Kate said.

The woman reached over her shoulder and pulled a plastic folder off a rack. "Right, right, honey. It was a mess, but Bill got it back together," the woman said, and looked over the papers in the folder. "It looks like between your dad and your insurance, all the charges are taken care of, so you don't have to pay a thing." She looked back up at Kate and smiled. A piece of paper slipped out of the file onto the counter. The redhead looked at it. "Oh right, one of the mechanics wants to talk to you."

"Is it about the car?" Kate asked.

"Yeah, probably." She stood and walked to a sliding door.

Kate looked to her right and saw the garage had six or seven stations, but only three with cars in them. Under the first car an Impala, nearest the door, she could see a pair of legs protrude from under it. The legs wore green pants and running shoes were on the feet.

The red-headed woman shouted, "Where's Bill?" Her voice wasn't loud enough to be heard over the noise that came from the garage. "Lord Almighty, I'll be right back, sweetie." The woman walked out and slid the door closed behind her.

Kate turned to the glass and watched the woman roam around the car stations. She walked between two vehicles toward the back. She'd apparently found who she looked for as she bent over the front of the car and pointed toward the office.

Kate found the garage interesting, but the smell of motor oil was awful. She didn't think she'd smell anything else for a while. As she watched, Kate saw a head with brown hair appear and nod as its owner stood up. The guy was really tall.

The woman started back to the office and when she walked in said, "Bill will be here in a second."

Kate continued to watch the garage. A mechanic in the corner banged on a piece of metal that looked like a bumper. The car closest to her had its bumper removed and the legs slid farther underneath. She put two and two together and figured out the bumper belonged to the Impala. She noticed a pair of blue coveralls walk toward the office and looked at the man in them. She started to turn her head, but stopped and almost snapped her neck looking back so fast. Her breath caught in her throat and she felt her eyes open wider. The tall, brown-haired man with blue eyes looked so very familiar. She backed up a step as he slid the glass door open. She began to feel every joint in her body turn to mush.

"Connor?" she whispered. She backed into the red-headed woman's desk.

The man looked at her and stopped in his tracks. He stared at her for a moment and smiled slightly. "Lizzie?" he said, loud enough for her to hear, then he took a step toward her.

Kate took another step sideways and got tangled with her cane. She fell over and landed hard on her arm and hip. Her head spun as she continued to watch the man approach her. He squatted down beside her, and asked if she was okay. She stared up at him and found the room getting very warm. Her mind was in a complete jumble. "How is this possible?" she whispered, again.

"Where have you been?" The man looked up at the redhead and cleared his throat.

"Miss, are you all right?" the redhead asked from behind the desk. She moved to a water cooler and got a cup for Kate.

Kate continued to stare at him. "Why did you call me Lizzie?" She took his hand and pushed herself up to stand.

"Sweetie, I think you should sit back down. You've gone awfully pale," the redhead said, and handed her the cup.

Kate realized the man still held her elbow. She didn't want him to let go and definitely didn't want to move her eyes away from him. She looked down at the water in her other hand, and then focused on the woman. "Thank you, I'm fine," she said, and then turned her attention back to the man. "You, apparently, needed to tell me something about my car."

"Your car?" He frowned.

"The 69 VW Beetle," Kate said, and raised her eyebrows. "Is there a problem?"

"VW...oh, right. No, there's no problem. I just...well, if you're ever interested in selling it, I'd like first chance to put in a bid. It's a terrific car."

"Thank you, but I don't think I'll get rid of it any time soon."

"If you ever do, I'm Bill Leary." He held his hand out to her. "Ah, could I buy you a cup of coffee? There's a Starbucks next door."

Kate slid hers into his grasp. "Kate Sullivan, and yes, I'd like a cup of coffee."

"Are you able to walk over there?" he asked and pointed at her cane.

"I'm a little slow, but I get there eventually."

Bill turned to the red-headed woman. "I'll be back in an hour or so," he said.

"I heard you. Why don't you let Ralph know?" Red asked and smirked.

"Let me wash my hands real quick. I'll be right back." He smiled at Kate.

She watched him disappear around a corner in the garage and couldn't believe she'd just accepted the offer of coffee. He looked so much like Connor, the man in her dream and he called her Lizzie. She couldn't wait to find out what he might know.

Chapter Four

After ten minutes, Bill Leary resurfaced. Not only had he washed his hands, but changed his clothes and combed his wavy brown hair. As he moved toward Kate, she looked him up and down. He wore jeans and a long sleeved T-shirt and he'd put on sneakers.

"See you tomorrow Paula." He waved at the woman behind the desk who continued to shake her head.

Kate followed him out of the garage. When they got to the sidewalk, she looked up at him and smiled.

"Did you hurt your leg in the accident?" he asked.

"No, not my leg, my hip was dislocated. Apparently, I tried to put my foot through the floorboard or something," she answered.

They went into the coffee shop and Bill turned to her. "What can I get for you?"

"Hmmm...I guess a tall iced Granita without whipped cream. Thank you."

"Okay, go find a place to sit and I'll be right there."

Kate watched him walk up to the counter, where there was a bit of a line. She saw a table by a window, hobbled over to it and sat down. She felt stunned by how much he looked like the man from her dream. His hair appeared to be a bit lighter brown, but that was the only difference. He moved just like Connor did.

He set her iced coffee down on the table and she looked up, as Bill sat down across from her.

"Thank you." She sipped the drink.

31

"So, why did you call me Connor?" he asked.

She sat back in her chair and smiled. "Why did you call me Lizzie?"

He looked down at his cup and chuckled. "I had a crazy feeling you'd say that, again." He handed her a napkin. "Write down the reason on the napkin and we'll reveal at the same time."

"That's fair." Kate pulled a pen out of her purse and scribbled one word on it. She looked up and saw he watched her closely.

"Ready?" he asked.

Kate nodded. They both held up the napkins for the other to see. They'd each written the same word. Dream.

She sat back, again. "Your hair is lighter brown, but you look just like him. You even have his blue eyes."

"You, too. You look just like Lizzie, except your blonde hair is darker and shorter. How long have you been having them? The dreams?"

"As long as I can remember. It was as though I grew up with her."

"Same here, except Connor grew up in Ireland," Bill said and took a sip of his coffee.

"That's right. He came over with his first wife. He lost her on the voyage."

"Her name was Fiona and Connor went through Ellis Island pretty much in shock. He lived in the slums in New York City for a while and then got a lucky break and headed west. He really hated New York. The gangs and racism really pissed him off. He couldn't stand being called Paddy."

"He mentioned something about an Irish gang trying to recruit him, but he didn't want anything to do with it. I can't remember the name of the guy who helped Connor, but he told me...I mean her..." Kate stopped and shook her head. "This is weird."

"His name was Fred Smalley. He was a good guy," Bill said.

"This is going to sound really strange, but I promise I'm not crazy. There have been times since the accident that I find it difficult to distinguish between her and me," she said.

Bill nodded and put his elbow on the table, with his chin in his hand. "That's happened to me, too. In fact... " He looked at her. "Never mind, it's not important."

"In fact, what?" Kate asked.

He smiled and laughed. "Even though we've only just met, I find you extremely attractive and feel like I've known you for a very long time. It's the now me that's having a problem. Now me? Yikes, that came out strange." He laughed at himself.

"I suppose I'm just as crazy then, because I understood completely what you meant." Kate laughed with him.

"Let's start over," Bill said, and sat up straighter in his chair. "I'm William Douglas Leary. My friends call me Bill. I'm going to be thirty in a couple of months. I'm a mechanic and, also teach at the community college. You guessed it; I teach auto shop. It's not as dull as it sounds. I was born in Everett and grew up in the area. I'm divorced. Hmmm...what else? Oh yeah, I like baseball. That's a start, now you go."

"I'm Kathryn Louise Sullivan. I turned twenty-six in April. I, too, was born in Everett, but raised in Seattle. It had something to do with my parents being at a dinner party and my mom going into labor a couple of weeks early. I work for social services at the university hospital. It can be dull, but I love to help people. I've never been married." She looked up at the ceiling. "I'm missing something. Oh, baseball is fine," she finished and smiled.

"I've known your dad for a few years. He's been bringing his car to our shop for as long as I can remember. He's a good man," he said and sat back.

"Yes, Dad's the best. Do your folks live in the area?"

"They divorced when I was ten. My mom remarried and they moved down to Arizona a few years ago. It's been a while since I talked to my dad. He moves around a lot. I asked him once if he knew much about the history of the Leary family, but he didn't have much information. He said something about an uncle who came over from Ireland. I did some genealogy research and found out that Connor was related to my grandfather." Bill shifted in his seat. "Back to the dreams...are you still having them?"

Kate looked at her hands. "After the accident, I was in the hospital, unconscious, for a couple of days. When I woke up the dream ended. I haven't had one since."

He stared at her. "When did you wake up?" he asked, quietly.

"September twenty-second."

He nodded and took his wallet out of his back pocket. "I haven't had a dream since then. In fact, I wrote the date down." He took out a folded piece of paper and handed it to her.

Kate slowly unfolded the paper and looked at the writing on it, 9/22/12. "Was it the wedding day dream?"

"With the fire, yes," he said. "The day they died."

She folded the paper up and handed it back to him, then put her hand up to her cheek and tried to get her eyes back in focus. She'd started to tear up. She closed her eyes. "And the fire," she whispered.

They went quiet for a few minutes, and she felt so surprised at his knowledge of the past events. They sat in the coffee house for three hours and discussed what they remembered about the dreams. Kate's cell phone vibrated in her jacket pocket, but she ignored it.

"Do you remember when we'd walk along the shoreline together?" he asked.

"*We?* I see you really do have the same problem keeping them separate from your own life."

Bill smiled and looked down at his cup. "Talk about a Freudian slip. Yeah, every now and then someone tells me I sound like I'm from Ireland. I pick up the accent sometimes."

Kate laughed. "I remember so much of their life; I sometimes wonder what's really my memories and what's theirs. What were you going to say about walking by the shore?"

"Oh, I just remember *Connor* and *Elizabeth* walking by the shore a lot." She heard him accentuate their names. "They'd follow paths all over West Seattle. Connor loved to watch her pick wildflowers during the summer when they picnicked. He didn't think it was possible to be so happy."

Chapter Five

Kate agreed with Bill when he said he couldn't remember a time when he didn't have the strange dreams. They'd had them ever since they were kids. Kate could never figure out why they came to her. They progressed every year as they grew up and very seldom changed. They both met all sorts of people in the dreams. Bill told her about the people Connor worked with in New York and those he'd met on the trip to the Northwest.

She told Bill that her dad had always been interested in the dreams and everything she could remember about them. Her mom always made her feel stupid whenever she mentioned them. She said Kate was being lazy and would never amount to anything if she day-dreamed her life away.

The one thing Kate wished she could remember was when the dreams started. All she knew was that they'd been with her just about all her life. A couple of days during any given month she would dream of this place from the past. They were like a serial story, the next one picked up where the last one left off. It was one of her first memories as a child. She recalled waking up and wondering why she was seeing television in the middle of the night. She'd asked her mom about it, who told her dreams were how her brain played while she slept. That didn't make much sense to her as a child, but it held for a while. As she grew older, she realized her mom found a nice way to explain something difficult to a youngster. She stopped believing in brains playing at around age twelve when puberty hit.

Bill agreed that he'd had them since childhood, too, but said he'd only told one other person. He'd never said a word to his parents. The one person was his ex-wife. There were other problems between them, but she got annoyed by the fact he dreamed of another woman. She claimed she could tell when he'd had one of the dreams, because he always woke up excited.

Bill commented about the way colors stood out, and Kate agreed. The usual panorama was pure blue sky with white fluffy clouds that floated by. Fields of farms wedged between huge cedar and madrona trees. Streams trickled into the water on the bay. It was their own private nature walk and each time they went there they woke up feeling calm and joyful.

As Kate grew older, the dream also seemed to grow. A small town showed up with dirt roads. People appeared and walked down the streets. The adults did their business and shopped and there were kids for her to play with. She'd walk down the middle of the road and look at the buildings. There was a general store, the sheriff's office, stables, a church and the boatyards. Horses with carts or by themselves were tied up along the street. People walked along the sidewalks past the stores dressed in strange clothes. At some point she realized she dreamt of a different time period.

Kate would wake up in the morning and run out to the kitchen to report her latest story to her dad. He'd sit and listen patiently with a smile on his face. She loved to tell him all about her latest dream and he let her imagination run wild. Her dad said, one day, she'd probably turn into a very good writer.

When she became a teenager, she learned not to mention anything about the dreams with her mom around. Maggie was the realist in the family. She hired a counselor for Kate and expected results. Her dad tried to be supportive and always listened. Her mom heard the stories and rolled her eyes. Once, her mom even asked if she planned to grow up as a

37

daydreamer. Kate replied that it wasn't a daydream, it was a night dream. She was only ten years old at the time. Her mom made it difficult to explore the dreams. She'd either make fun of Kate or call her names, so she decided it would be best to keep the dreams to herself. If she was alone with her dad, she still talked about them, but kept silent for the most part.

When she turned twelve, puberty set in and the dream changed again. It seemed as though when Kate changed, the dream changed, too. Around that time, the people in the dream began to talk to her. She'd walk down a street, and the men tipped their hats and said, "Good day Miss Elizabeth." She knew her name was Kate, but also knew she was in another time.

As she approached the General Store she saw her reflection in the window. She wore a long skirt and a blouse with long sleeves buttoned half way up to her elbow. Her hair was piled on top of her head with a small hat pinned to it. She knew it wasn't her era. Her hair was cut at the shoulders and usually a mess.

In her middle teens, Kate realized she knew things that hadn't appeared in the dreams. She knew Elizabeth had three sisters. Delia was the oldest, then Elizabeth. Effie was a year or two younger than she and the littlest, Winonna, was several years younger. Their father worked for a mortgage and loan company and did volunteer work for the YMCA. Their mother was a housewife and helped out at the Methodist Church. But how Kate knew all of these things, remained a mystery to her.

Kate's mom and dad were born and raised in Washington State. They met when they attended West Seattle High School. When her dad finished undergraduate work at the University of Washington, he studied business and finance and got his masters degree. He couldn't decide if he wanted to teach or work for a stock trading company. The latter became his choice and he did pretty well with the markets. Later, he'd been offered positions to teach at schools around the country, but the one thing her parents agreed on was that neither of them wanted to leave the Northwest. Kate found out many years later that once her dad was offered a position in Boston, but turned it down. She asked him about it and he said, "I wasn't ready to give up saltwater, rain and fish. I know they have fish back east, but it just isn't as good as the salmon we get from Puget Sound."

Kate's mom became a travel agent and housewife. She took very good care of their home and child. She also spent time with the Women's Auxiliary and Volunteer services at a local hospital. She loved to arrange dinner parties in honor of anything that moved.

When Kate turned seventeen, her grandmother came to live with them. She was in her middle eighties and having a difficult time living on her own. Her memory at times was a little sketchy. Kate's dad wouldn't discuss moving her to a nursing home. Her mom didn't like the idea, but against her wishes, her mother-in-law moved in with them. She was a dear lady who always seemed to smell of lavender. She would sneak treats into her room for Kate and always seemed to have a jar full of jellybeans. Kate called her Grammy and loved her very much. Her mom refused to help care for Grammy, so her dad hired daytime helpers to keep an eye on her.

On one of her grandmother's clearer moments, she told Kate that she looked just like her sister Elizabeth. It startled Kate and she suddenly remembered that her grandmother's name was Winonna. She tried to ask questions about Elizabeth, but Grammy became vague and angry. She said that Elizabeth died sometime ago, but wouldn't say anymore. It was a long time before Kate brought Elizabeth up again.

Discovering all this bothered Kate and she talked to her dad about it. He said he remembered hearing about another sister who died tragically around the turn of the century, but didn't know much more.

Kate went to the city library and looked at books that discussed dreams and the afterlife. She also looked at old microfiche of newspapers and magazines. She could never really find the answers. She continued to have the dream, but was no longer comfortable with it. She finally set her research aside, and decided she needed to concentrate on her studies.

A few years later, Kate left Seattle to go to college. She crossed over the mountains to the eastern part of the state and went to Gonzaga University in Spokane. She came home at Christmas and spring break to spend time with the family, but enjoyed being on her own. She also met Henry Parsons. After graduation, they moved into a townhome together in Seattle. Her mother asked on several different occasions when she and Henry were going to get married. Kate tried a couple of times to discuss the subject, but nothing developed and Henry didn't seem very interested. That was five years ago.

The dream continued to expand as she grew older. There came a point when Kate realized that Elizabeth was being courted by someone. His name was Connor O'Leary. He arrived in town a few months before she met him from the New York area. He bought into a partnership at one of the stables in town with money he'd worked hard to earn. He loved the work with horses and did just about everything to care for them. He worked as a blacksmith and shoed horses. He was reliable and after a time, people knew his name and brought problem horses to him and no one else.

Elizabeth would find him hard at work in the stables, but Connor always found time for her. He was tall with strong arms and shoulders, dark hair and blue eyes and she loved to watch him work. He'd be shoeing a horse or cleaning a stall, but when Elizabeth walked up he would immediately stop the task at hand. He'd get cleaned up and come to say "hello."

They strolled down the city streets, and smiled at one another, or walked to the park by the bay and had a picnic under a tree. If the weather was poor, they would have lunch in the stables or schoolhouse where Elizabeth taught. After a time, Kate realized Elizabeth was in love and very happy.

Elizabeth's younger sister, Effie, sometimes trailed after them and it became apparent that she was very jealous of the love that grew between the couple. Elizabeth knew Effie had developed a crush on Connor and tried to talk to her about it. Effie wouldn't sit still and listen. She'd leave the room before a discussion could get started. There were family dinners when Effie loudly commented that she saw Elizabeth and Connor kiss. Elizabeth's father would look at his daughter with disapproval and end the subject.

"I'm sorry, Bill. I'm monopolizing the conversation," Kate said.

"No, you're not. I love hearing your memories of the dreams. I never knew much about Lizzie's childhood." He smiled.

"I didn't mean to go into all my family history though."

"That's an added benefit. I get to know more about you, too." He winked at her.

"Okay, then, where was I? During that time in the dreams, it was really hard to figure out if I dreamt of someone else or myself. When I was home from school I'd try to discuss it with Grammy, but I never got very far. Grammy didn't like to talk about her sister or my mom would enter the room. I didn't want her to know I still had the dreams." Kate looked at her empty cup of iced coffee.

"Do you want another coffee?" Bill asked.

"No." She took in a breath. "I graduated with a degree in Social Work and began to work at the University Hospital. Henry keeps busy at work and does pretty well with the stock market. He signed on as my dad's student assistant and I think he considers himself to be my dad's understudy." Kate looked across the table at Bill and thought it would be best not to go into all of the mess with Henry. "And in a blink of an eye, four years passed. I haven't done much research into the dream world since," she finished her monolog.

Kate thought about Henry and knew she had to make a move sooner than later. They did talk once about getting married, but found it wasn't very important to either one of them. Henry was a decent enough man, but Kate didn't feel she really loved him. She would spend a few sleepless nights trying to decide whether or not to break it off. She'd then get distracted by work and time would slip by again.

They enjoyed each other's company and Kate thought it was nice to have someone to say hello to when she came home. She never felt as though she could be completely honest with him and never told him about the dreams. One night at dinner with her parents, her mom brought up this funny story about the insane dreams Kate talked about when she was a child. She explained to Henry that Kate had quite the imagination when she was young. She thought Kate had out-grown them in her teens. She and Henry laughed until tears ran down their cheeks. Kate felt embarrassed and glad she'd stopped talking about them in front of her mom. At the time, if her mom discovered that Kate still had the dreams, she might have wound up in a sanitarium.

Friends asked many times why she didn't find another guy or settle down with Henry. It was hard for her to explain, but she waited for one particular man. It was a long story.

Kate always felt that if God meant for him to show up, He would make it happen. She continued to read books about dream subjects and relationships until her eyes crossed. In her heart, she knew it was only a dream.

"Do you remember a guy named Ben something? I can't remember his last name," Bill asked.

She looked over at Bill and smiled. "Yeah, I remember Ben Harley. He was a pain in Lizzie's backside. He wanted to court her like crazy, and even proposed, but she never took him seriously. He gave up at some point."

"He really gave Connor an earful one morning. He stormed into the iron works and said Connor was to keep away from Miss Elizabeth. Apparently, Ben felt she was already spoken for and tried to threaten him. Connor was a strong man, and it didn't take much to get Ben to back off. The creep really was sour when they announced their engagement."

"I think Lizzie was so happy about getting married that she didn't register anything Ben said to her about Connor." Kate sighed and sat back in her chair. "Now I know it was more than a dream really, because here you are and you understand what I'm talking about. Weird."

Bill looked at her again with an easy smile. "Kate, we've been sitting here for a couple of hours and if I don't get my butt off this hard seat soon I won't be able to walk. Would you like to get some lunch?" he asked and stood up.

"I've been doing most of the talking, too. I'm sorry, but it's really nice to have someone to discuss this with who understands." She looked at her watch, surprised to see it was after three in the afternoon. "Sure, lunch sounds great. I still have to get my car."

Bill pulled a set of keys out of his pocket and held them up. "I think these are yours." He handed the keys to her.

"Okay, if you'll point out where my car is, I can go get it," she said and slowly got up.

"Why don't we carpool somewhere together? Your car's parked over on the side of the building. I can drop you back there later."

"I could always follow you in my car and save you the trip back," she said. They walked out of the coffee shop.

"But then you wouldn't get to ride in my manly truck." Bill grinned at her.

"Baseball and manly trucks, eh?"

"Yes ma'am, nothing but top grade testosterone here," he said.

Kate laughed and agreed to ride in the truck. He helped her up into the truck. The step was higher than she thought it would be and she found it difficult to push up with her left leg. Her right hip wasn't as flexible or strong as it used to be.

They went to late lunch-early dinner at a seafood restaurant on the waterfront in Everett. After they finished their meal, they strolled around the docks and parks, and continued to talk about the dream and about themselves. Kate felt relaxed and grateful to have someone she could talk to about the strange night-time visions.

Chapter Six

Kate walked into her parents' kitchen after eight in the evening. She found her mom and dad at the kitchen table with Henry.

"Where have you been?" her mom asked, and sounded a bit annoyed.

"I spent the day with a friend and we had dinner out. I'm over eighteen, Mom, I don't have to report in," Kate said.

Henry stood up and went to give her a hug. "Hey, babe."

"Hey." She tried to smile and sat down at the table next to her dad.

"Next time, just call to let us know you're all right, please," Maggie Sullivan continued.

"Sure," Kate said. Her dad nudged her knee under the table and she winked at him.

"You must have your cell phone turned off. I've been trying to call all afternoon," Henry said.

"Sorry, I didn't even think about it."

"Who did you see?" Henry asked.

She looked at him across the table and realized she hardly knew him anymore. "Someone I haven't seen for a long time. It's no one you've ever met."

"Did you go to school with her?" Maggie asked.

Kate looked at her mom, and tried not to get sour. "No, I didn't go to school with him. Mom and Dad, I need to talk to Henry." She stood back up and walked toward the back door. "Let's go outside where we might find some privacy." She felt tired from the day, but it was a nice tired. Even in physical therapy she hadn't walked as much, as she did today with Bill.

She sat on a picnic table bench and Henry leaned against the deck railing. Kate held her cane in front of her and spun it in circles. Finally, she looked up at him. "Why did you tell my mom that I was driving the car the night of the accident? Why did you tell our friends that?"

"I don't remember telling that to anyone, Kate. Besides, haven't we already discussed this? Seems like you've already reamed me out for that and I explained," he replied and rested his elbows on the rail.

"Ah, yes, selective memory. I forgot you have a degree in that," she said, and looked at the back of her cane. "Funny, you remember the discussion."

"What's that supposed to mean?"

"Nothing, nothing at all. It's just that I don't appreciate being lied to."

"Babe, when are you coming home? I miss you," Henry said, and ignored her statement.

She looked up at him and remembered when they'd first met. They'd been two juniors, working toward a degree. They'd been together for five years, but she'd been thinking of breaking it off for over two years. She felt angry at herself for not getting down to business sooner.

"I'm not coming back, Henry. I'll be by to pack up my stuff, but, no, I'm not coming back," she said.

He looked at her in surprise. "You're blaming me for the accident? Those teens were as drunk, if not drunker, than I was," he said and pushed away from the rail. He squatted in front of her and put his hands on her thighs.

"It has nothing to do with the accident," she said.

"Then what? What is your problem?"

"What is my problem? See, Henry, that right there is the problem. As a couple aren't we supposed to work on our problems together? It always seems to me, I'm the one who causes the trouble."

"You know that's not what I meant."

"I'm tired." Kate scratched her scalp. "I'm tired of feeling like I'm the only one doing any of the work on this relationship. Somewhere, we lost track of each other. We don't talk anymore, you shut me off with how silly I am and I'm through trying. I have no energy left to deal with us anymore."

Henry tightened his hold on her legs. "We're talking now. What do you want to say?"

Kate raised her hands. "Nothing, I have nothing more to say but that I'm finished. It's time to move on. I'll be by next week to pack up."

"So that's it? You're just cutting me off and I don't get a chance to defend myself?"

"There's nothing to defend. We've grown apart and we both need to move on." She moved his hands and stood up. She started to move toward the back door. "Goodnight, Henry."

"This isn't over, Kate. I still want to understand why," he said to her back as she closed the door to the house. He pushed the door open and followed her into kitchen. He grabbed her arm hard and spun her around to face him. "Don't turn your back on me. I haven't put all this time into this relationship to have it just shut off." He held her arms tight.

"Henry, you're hurting my arm, let go." Kate tried to get him to release her.

"Just like you're hurting me," he spat, and pushed her against the kitchen counter.

"Let her go Henry," she heard a deep, angry voice say. Her dad stood in the opposite doorway.

Henry looked at him and released her arms. She limped to her dad, who moved her behind him. "I think you need to go home now. I hope some rest will help you think more clearly."

Henry nodded and turned to the back door. "I'm not giving up Kate," he said as he left the house.

Kate put her hand on her dad's shoulder, as he turned. "Thanks, Pop."

"You're welcome, sweetheart. Would you like to explain to me what just happened?" he asked and led her to the kitchen table.

"Where's Mom?" she asked and sat down.

"She went upstairs to do some reading," he answered. He poured two cups of coffee and set one in front of his daughter.

"First of all, Henry and I are breaking up or I just broke up with him. I can't stand it anymore and it's time to end the relationship. I'll go over to start packing things up next week and try to find a place to live. I know Mom won't be happy..."

"Don't worry about your mom. I'll explain it to her and find a way for her to understand," Ian said.

"Dad, remember when I woke up in the hospital and said they died and everyone thought I was talking about the teenagers in the car?" She watched him nod his head. "How do I explain this? The two people from the dream were the ones who died ... crap, I already told you that. To top everything off, I met the man from the dream today. He was one of the mechanics at the auto shop; you know him and have probably known him for years. He said you've been bringing your car to them for a long time. I almost fainted when I first saw him. He looks just like the man from that dream I've been having forever."

"There are a couple of mechanic's I deal with, Kate," he said.

"He's tall - six-foot-four - at least, brown hair, blue eyes. His name is Bill."

He raised his eyebrows and tilted his head. "I don't really notice hair color. Wait a minute... Bill? He's been with that garage since he was a kid."

"I'm glad you don't notice men, Dad, and yes, I mean Bill." She saw him press his lips together. "Anyway, I spent the afternoon and evening with him talking and comparing notes. He seems to know a lot about these types of dreams. He's been having the same dreams, too. He said I look just like the woman in them."

"You don't think this guy could somehow be scamming you?" her father asked and sounded concerned.

"No way. You're the only one I've ever told any of the adult portions and details to. I doubt very much you would tell the neighbors or some mechanic in an auto shop," she said, and arched her brow.

"No sweetheart, I can't think of anyone I said anything to." His brows came together. "Bill's worked on my cars and your mom's car a couple of times. He seems very down to earth and honest. He pretty much said that one of the cars was going to nickel and dime us to death with repairs," he said and laughed.

"Dad, I don't want to change the subject, but he knows details about Lizzie and Connor that no one knew anything about. He remembered the fire and things that went on before that. He even stopped having the dreams the same day I woke up in the hospital. He wrote the date down. It was so amazing to talk to him."

Ian frowned. "Fire? I remember you talked about that when you woke up, but now that you're giving names it sounds really familiar. I thought you were remembering the accident."

"What?"

"Kate, was Connor's last name Leary?"

"Yes, only it was O'Leary."

Her dad stood up and held out his hand. "Come with me."

Chapter Seven

Kate and her dad made their way up the stairs to the second floor of the family home. Then her dad walked to the end of the hall and pulled a rope which brought the attic stairs down from the ceiling.

Kate's mother looked out the master bedroom door. "What are you two doing?" she asked.

"Go back to your book, Maggie. We're just looking for something," He answered and started up the stairs. "Be careful, Kate. I don't want you to break anything else."

He pulled a string and turned on the overhead lights and began to look at the boxes that accumulated over the years. "I'll never understand why your mother feels this stuff is worth hanging on to. It just gathers dust."

"What are you looking for dad?" Kate asked from the edge of the stairwell.

"There was an old steamer trunk that belonged to your grandmother's family, with mostly old photo's and letters, but there was some other stuff in it, too. I remember a long time ago when I was a kid, I overheard a discussion my mom was having with her sister Delia. They mentioned a fire. When my mom started to call you Lizzie, I should have put it all together. I guess I was slow on picking up the puzzle pieces. There's the trunk," he said, and moved a stack of boxes. He pulled an old chest away from the wall, and lifted the lid. "Here we go. Pull up a chair, sweetheart. You did know your grandma's older sister was named Elizabeth?"

"Yeah, when she started calling me that name and said I looked so much like her... it was a while before I realized it was

51

the woman from the dream. I thought once all of this might have to do with reincarnation, but I couldn't figure it out. I was in school and didn't really have the time to think about it."

Her dad pulled a folder out of the trunk and looked through it, then pulled out one page and handed it to Kate.

"You might find this of interest," he said and turned back to the trunk.

She looked at the paper. It was an old marriage license and her brain froze."Oh my God," she whispered. The bride and groom were Elizabeth Mary MacDiarmid and Connor James O'Leary.

"I never knew my Aunt Lizzie. Mom was ten or eleven when they died in a hotel fire," her dad said, and watched her closely. He handed her a dark brown folder and put his hand over hers before she could look inside. "Kate, I've never believed in this reincarnation business. I always thought it was mumbo-jumbo, but now I'm not so certain."

She looked at the envelope and saw gold lettering with the name of some old photo studio, and ran her fingers over it. She looked up at her dad. Her eyebrows came together. "Dad?"

He nodded and smiled. "Look at the pictures and tell me what you think. I believe they were taken the day of their wedding."

She opened the folder and revealed a black and white photograph of Lizzie and Connor. He was seated in a small frame chair. She stood behind him with her hand on his shoulder. They both smiled. Connor wore a dark suit, with what seemed like an overly large collar. Elizabeth had on a white gown that looked to be made mostly of lace. It was beautiful.

"My Lord, Dad, I remember this. The photographer used a very old camera and he told us that we couldn't hold a smile as long as the shutter needed to stay open. We sat that way for a minute or more. I wasn't about to not smile for the most important pictures of my life. It was the happiest day," her voice faded as her fingers moved over the photo.

"Here's another, Kate." He handed her another brown folder. It was another portrait taken closer to the bride and groom. Both still smiled.

"It was the first time I sat on his lap," she said quietly.

"Sweetheart, you keep saying 'I' and 'we'. You weren't there," he said.

She looked up at him again confused. She could see the concerned look on his face. "I have to go." She stood up.

"Go? You just got home and it's late. It's after 9:00," her dad said, and looked at his watch.

"Dad, there's no way I'll be able to sleep tonight. I have got to show these to Bill." She started to move to the stairs.

"Kate, drive carefully, please."

"I will Dad." She turned and looked up the stairs at him. "Thanks for this. I don't feel quite so crazy anymore."

"You've never been crazy. Be careful," he said.

"Night, Dad." She turned and went back through the kitchen. She grabbed her purse and cell phone on the way. She put the license and pictures in her bag and pulled out her car keys. She climbed into the front of the restored VW, pulled her cell phone out of her purse and hit the speed dial button by Bill Leary's name.

It rang several times and then he answered. "Hello?"

"Bill, this is Kate. I know it's late and I'm sorry if I woke you..." She put the keys in the ignition and started the car.

"I'm not sorry. I was scrunched on the couch in the wrong position. I would have woken up with a stiff neck," he said, through a yawn. "What's up?"

"I have some things I need to show you. I don't want you to think I'm stalking you, but I've waited twenty-six years to find someone I could discuss this with. You have to see what my dad gave to me tonight. It's totally amazing," she said and backed out of the driveway to the road.

"Kate, you can stalk me anyplace, anytime. Do you know how to get to Highwood?"

"I know its north, but I don't go all the way to Lynnwood."

Bill gave her directions and said he'd put on the coffee. She tried not to speed when she got onto the freeway, but it was hard not to. She thought about the pictures and wondered why she'd never seen them before. She'd been up in that attic a million times and played up there as a kid. Then she realized her grandmother hadn't moved in until Kate was older and as a teenager she hadn't played in the attic.

***

He sat in his car parked under a tree at the end of the Sullivan's street. Henry wanted to continue the discussion with Kate, but his anger got the better of him. They would just have to finish the conversation at another time.

Henry wanted to tell her everything, but found it difficult. When he'd first seen Kate in college he'd nearly had a stroke. Who would have thought after all these years, destiny would bring them back together. She was meant to be his from the start, but the situation proved to be wrong. He hadn't meant for her to get hurt. The fire was only supposed to kill him.

He heard an engine fire up and a few seconds later Kate's VW flew past his car. He started his engine and began to follow her, wondering where she was going this late at night.

***

Kate remembered everything about the day those pictures were taken. It was so wonderful. That photographer argued with her - or rather, Lizzie - about not smiling. She guessed it was why, in so many of the old time pictures, the

54

people posed with frowns on their faces. She felt happy that Lizzie and Connor smiled. It made the picture much warmer.

Kate got off the freeway and followed Bill's directions. She slowed down and paid closer attention to her driving, when she blew through a four-way stop. She turned onto his street and followed the house numbers. She found a mailbox shaped like a '61 Mustang. Apparently, Bill Leary really liked cars, which caused Kate to smile. "He and Dad will have something to talk about," she mumbled as she found the driveway.

She pulled up to a one story rambler, and saw the front porch light come on and the door open. She grabbed her purse and got out of the car.

***

Henry saw her car slow down and then swing into a driveway. When he saw the front door open and the man come out, he stopped his car. He turned off his lights and just stared at the man.

"Son-of-a-bitch," he hissed. "Where the hell did you come from?"

Chapter Eight

"Hi, Bill. My dad decided to be very helpful tonight. He's always been supportive, which I guess I told you earlier. Anyway, there's a steamer trunk in my parents' attic which belongs my grandmother. Grammy also lives with my parents. She was Lizzie's youngest sister, Winonna." She rambled on as she breezed by him and walked into his front hallway. She turned to look at him when she realized she didn't have a clue which way to go. "Sorry, I didn't mean to steam right past you there. Patience isn't a strong trait in my family."

"No problem, it's good to see you, again. It seems like ages since we last talked." He shut the door behind him and pointed to the right. "The kitchen's that way."

Kate followed his pointed finger and found a huge, well-thought-out room. She admired the cabinets and island. The floor appeared a little dark, but the rest of the room felt warm and inviting.

"Let me guess, you're married?" she said.

"Divorced. I mentioned it earlier, and my ex never lived here. Some of the fixtures and color scheme is from the previous owners' do-it-yourself days. I'm going to make changes sometime, but haven't gotten to it yet."

"It's nice," she said.

"Coffee?"

"Yes, that's a good idea." She saw the kitchen table and moved to it. She watched him pour the cups of coffee. His T-shirt was pulled out of his jeans and wrinkled around his rear. She smiled as he put a cup in front of her.

"So, what did your father give you?" He sat in the chair next to her.

Kate pulled the two folders and license out of her bag. "First, there's this. It's Elizabeth and Connor's marriage license." She handed it to him.

Bill looked at it and nodded. "I remember when they signed this. June 23, 1912. They've been married 100 years. What do you know? I don't know if I was aware of the date."

She handed him the first photograph. Bill sat up straight.

"Hey, I remember this, too. You argued with the photographer about smiling. It had something to do with the shutter being open too long," he said and looked at the picture. "I hated that tie so much."

Kate opened the second one and put it into his hands. "When my dad showed me this one I said it was the first time ..."

"You sat on my lap." He looked at her and frowned. "Or *she* sat...wait, I'm getting mixed up."

"Right, I said I sat on his lap. So we're equal in the confusion area and getting worse. I don't know if this will make any sense, but I don't know if these memories are mine or hers. I don't know if I was there or have been possessed or haunted all my life by this other person. I do know for certain she was my grandmother's sister. I'm also willing to bet that you're having the same feeling or have at least thought of it that way at some point in your life." She held her hands flat. "Possessed, haunted or reincarnated?" She moved her hands up and down. "Why is it Leary and not O'Leary?" She sat back and took a sip of coffee.

"You noticed that, eh?" He smirked and raised his eyebrows. "Back in the 1960's, my dad apparently thought it would be great if people thought he was related to Timothy Leary. He dropped the O and pissed my granddad off royally. I've thought about putting it back but never got around to it.

The amount of paperwork needed to change your name is incredible. I have a very big *Need to Do* file." He rested his elbow on the table and put his chin in his hand. "These are amazing. I'm sure if someone looked at them they'd think the pictures had been staged and processed somehow."

"Yeah, I always wear my hair up in a bun." She gathered her hair at the nape of her neck and smiled.

"And a tie always comes in handy at the garage." He laughed and looked at her. "I like your hair better down. No, wait...Connor preferred Lizzie to wear her hair down," he said and pressed his lips together. "There I go, again."

"Bill, seriously, a few years ago I thought about doing regression hypnosis to see if any of this could be sorted out. I got side-tracked with college and never tried it, but I'm thinking about it again. Have you ever thought of doing anything like hypnosis?"

"No, not really. I did some reading on past lives and dreams; some were interesting and some more Hollywood commercial." He looked at her over the edge of his cup and sipped his coffee.

"It's a bit scary not being in control with the hypnosis. I mean who wants to bark like a dog?" she said.

Bill smiled. "Woof." He set his cup down. "Would you be interested in trying it? I think it might help us both find out more."

"Yes, it would be helpful," Kate said and thought for a moment.

"You're frowning, what's the matter?" he asked.

She looked at him and found it baffling how comfortable she felt talking to him. "Remember I mentioned to you earlier about my boyfriend and I breaking up? I did it this evening. We've lived together for a couple of years and all the information I have about hypnosis is in my desk at the townhouse." She sat back. "I do have the names of a couple of

58

doctors recently given to me when I was in the hospital, but I still need to go over to the house and pack. I could try to find that information then."

"Is there any reason to worry about your safety? He wouldn't try to hurt you would he? I suddenly feel a strong urge to protect you."

"Thank you, but I don't think Henry would do anything. He's never hurt me in the past. It should go okay." She smiled slightly.

"Remember what you said about being confused? Since looking at these pictures..." Bill stopped and shook his head. "It's all I can do to keep from pulling you onto my lap and just holding on. It's really a strong feeling, too and, as you said, I'm not sure if *I'm* feeling this or if it's coming from Connor."

"It is weird and I think the more we get sorted out the better. We can't just leave it hanging." Kate looked at her watch. "Yikes, it's after midnight." She stood and took her cup to the sink.

"Tomorrow is Saturday and I can put off my class prep until Sunday. I could be freed up all day, if you'd want me to go with you to get the hypnosis information." He stood.

"Don't you work fixing cars and all that?" She walked back to the table and picked up her bag.

"Ralph, the owner of the garage, and I have an agreement. I work if I'm there. He's known me since I was a bratty kid and taught me everything I know about cars. He tolerates me pretty well. I also own part of the place, so he can't fire me," Bill chuckled.

"That's a definite in." Kate moved back toward the front door.

"Do you want to leave the pictures?" he asked and followed her to the door.

Kate turned around smiling and walked backwards out the door. "It gives me an excuse to come back."

"You are stalking me," he said, and stepped over the threshold.

"I am not." She turned back around and stopped at her car door. "You're the one following me."

Bill kept moving and gently bumped his body against hers. He backed her into the car, and put his hands on either side of her face. She felt him trace her lower lip with his thumb. She moved her hands onto his waist, as he looked down into her eyes.

"I've got to know," he whispered. He leaned his head down, and lightly put his lips against hers. She parted them and allowed his tongue easy entrance. The warmth spread through her body as he kissed around her mouth and nibbled on her lower lip. She felt his hands move down to her waist, and he lifted her off her feet and pressed her against the car. Their faces were even and Kate moved to Bill's ear and licked his lobe.

She straightened up and opened her eyes. "This is interesting. How'd you learn to kiss so well?"

"Back seat of my stepdad's Ford in high school with a girl named Rachel. I think she went on to be a middle school teacher. Damn, I never felt anything like this before. You're making me...well, I think you get the picture."

Kate could feel his hard penis pressed against the front of her thigh. "Not only do I get the picture, but I feel it, too." She moved her leg slightly back against him. "That's my good leg. If you don't want me to know, press against the other leg. I'm still getting the feeling back." She kissed and bit his chin and jawline.

"It doesn't annoy you? We haven't even known each other for twenty-four hours - although, we might have known each other for over 100 years."

She pulled her head back again. "What annoys me?"

"My more than obvious excitement."

"Oh sure, yeah, I'm way annoyed. In fact, I can't think of anything more annoying. How could you..."

He cut her off and pressed his lips against hers. He swept her mouth with his tongue. She put her hands around his neck and twirled her tongue against his.

He kissed along her jaw and asked, "Where is your cane?"

"Oh," She had to think for a second. "It's probably still up in the attic. I didn't even think about it when I left."

His lips pressed against hers again and they kissed for several minutes. Bill finally let her slide down and set her gently back on the ground.

"That kiss is going to give me excellent dreams tonight." He sighed.

Kate looked up at him and held onto his arms. "Me, too. I think you'll be the one appearing in them."

"Good. I'll call you tomorrow. Have dinner with me?" He put his hand up to her face and pushed her hair behind her ear.

"Okay, this one is on me though. You bought earlier tonight, so tomorrow is my turn," she said and arched her brow.

"Are you likely to argue with me?" He smiled.

Kate put on her best shocked expression. "Dude, I'm the lover-not-a-fighter cliché. I also believe in equality."

"No barefoot in the kitchen for you?"

"I've been shoeless in the kitchen before, but not like what I think you mean," she said. "Are you planning to let me go anytime soon?"

"Nope." He grinned.

"So you're just going to keep rubbing your manly self against me, annoying me all over the place?"

"Yep."

"What did you mean?" she asked and saw a confused look come over his face. "Before the first kiss, you said *I have to know?*"

Bill grinned again. "Right, coffee, you tasted like coffee."

"You had to know what I tasted like? That is mighty weird. Just for the record though, you tasted like coffee, too, and it was better than morning mouth."

Bill made a face and stuck out his tongue. "That is gross." He adjusted his groin and kissed her forehead. "We could go on like this all night, I think."

"Yeah, but I don't have to work tomorrow and you do. I get to sleep in." She smiled.

"Bing...wrong answer. Tomorrow is Saturday. I get to sleep in, too. I'll see you tomorrow. Early in the morning works great for me, if you don't want to wait until later in the day. We could have breakfast." Bill kissed her one more time and reluctantly let Kate go.

She got into her car and looked up at him. "Cripes, this has messed up my brain so much I can't even keep track of what day of the week it is, let alone what I'm having for breakfast. Good-night," she said and backed the car out of his driveway.

***

As Henry watched them kiss, he felt his anger rise again. He couldn't believe what he saw. *That tall, asshole is stealing my woman, again, and she seems to be tempting him.* Kate had turned into a slut and he'd need to nip this in the bud. His mind blazed as though it was on fire. Maybe they were already fucking and that was why she broke up with him. He needed to do something real quick before he lost her again.

Chapter Nine

The next morning Kate woke up with more energy than she'd felt in weeks. After she got cleaned up, she went to her parents' kitchen and found her mom at the table with a cup of coffee and the morning newspaper.

"Morning, Mom. Where's Dad?" Kate asked and poured a cup of coffee.

"He went into the office early to do some work on a new project. He thinks he'll be home for lunch, but, knowing him, we probably won't see him until dinner. I have to go into the agency and do some work, too. I just don't need to be there until eleven. So much for Saturday," her mom said and put the paper down. "Where did you drive off to last night?"

Kate pinched her lips together and wondered what she should tell her mother. She sat down at the table. "Well, see...I'm seeing a new man. I mean I think we're seeing each other," she said and shook her head. "Mom, I broke it off with Henry last night and..."

"I know, your father told me," Maggie said and smirked.

"Right, Dad said he was going to tell you. The new man's name is Bill Leary..."

"And he's a mechanic," her mom said flatly.

"Yeah, he works on cars, but he also teaches at the community college. He's pretty smart, Mom," Kate said and tried not to get angry.

"Is he the reason you're giving up on Henry?"

"No."

"How long have you been seeing him?"

"We met yesterday and ..." Kate looked at her mom and knew there was no getting through to her. Maggie Sullivan frowned deeply and had a look in her eyes that Kate knew all too well. "Never mind, it's not important."

"I thought you said you had dinner with a friend you had known for a long time? Now, you say you just met yesterday?" Her mom's eyebrows went up.

Kate realized she was going to back herself into a corner with this discussion. "I have known him for a long time...oh Mom, it's a complicated story."

"Sweetheart, just don't rush into anything. Think about the years you've spent with Henry and how much more he is able to provide for you than this garage mechanic," her mom said.

"There are things between Henry and me that you have no knowledge of, Mom. Were you aware that the Labor Day accident wasn't the first time he's been too drunk to drive, but did it anyway?"

"Shouldn't you be supporting him with this drinking issue?" Maggie sat back and still frowned. "Relationships mean you help your partner, not run out when the going gets tough."

"Mom, I have tried a million times to discuss it with Henry, but he doesn't think he has a problem. Doesn't it mean anything to you that he could have gotten me killed in that accident?" Kate rose from the table and started to leave the room.

"Of course it means something to me, Kate. How could you think that?"

Kate turned slowly around and leaned against the door jamb. "Mom, there are more problems and believe me, I've tried to deal with them. Henry doesn't see it that way and if he's not willing to put work into the relationship, then why should I?"

Her mom started to say something, but there was a knock on the back door. It swung open and Henry put his head in.

"Hi there, I'm not interrupting anything am I?" he asked and smiled. He walked in and shut the door behind him. He moved toward Kate, put his arm around her waist and asked. "When are you coming home?"

She looked at him and asked him twice to repeat it. He wanted to know when she was coming home. "I thought I made it clear to you last night that I wasn't coming back, but you must have missed something. Henry, this isn't the right time to discuss this," she said, as she moved away from him and sat down at the table next to her mom.

"So, when would the right time be?" Henry asked.

"I think I'd better let you two talk. I'll be upstairs if you need me Kate," Maggie said and left the room in a hurry.

"Henry, look, I know we should have talked more about this last night, and, oh, I don't know when a right time would be. No time like the present right?"

Henry sat down at the table. "Right."

"I'm not coming back to you or the townhouse. I'm going to start looking for a place of my own. I'll only be coming by to pack up my things," Kate said plainly.

Henry looked down at the floor. "You know the car crash wasn't my fault. Those kids had more to drink than I did. When are you going to forgive me for the accident?"

"It's not a matter of forgiveness, Henry. I blame everyone involved with that. You, me, and those kids. All of us were at fault. I particularly blame me. I should never have let you drive that night. I should never have gotten into the car with you. Do you even remember discussing this last night?"

"Yeah, but I hoped you might change your mind. What can I do to help you come back to me?" Henry said, and shredded a napkin.

"Henry..."

"It's him isn't it? I've been fighting against his type for years," he said so quietly she almost didn't hear him.

"Him, who?"

"That man you went to last night."

"You followed me?" she asked, and stood up.

"Yeah, I followed you. Did you fuck him?" He looked up at her.

Kate was surprised by that. "I'm not even going to answer that question. Henry, you and I have been growing apart for a long time. I've been mulling this over for months, but it never seemed like the right time to bring it up. For me, now is the right time to end it. I said it last night. It's time to move on with our lives," she said flatly.

"Is it that easy for you to give up our lives together?" he asked. "I care very much for you, Kate. I don't think we should throw away everything we've built."

"See, caring is very nice, but I'm looking for love. I'm looking for settling down. And what have we built? You get drunk all the time and we don't really have anything resembling a home," she said.

"When we discussed this before you said settling down wasn't on your agenda. Now suddenly it's important? Now you want a home and a yard to take up all your time? I suppose you even want kids."

"Henry, it's not so suddenly. As I said, I've been mulling things over for the last couple of months. If we had a healthy relationship, I would have discussed this with you, but we don't talk, unless its superficial things, or what party we're going to or where do we want to go for dinner. I want more than that and I'm sorry, I don't think that's where you're at, right now. Can we meet at the house tomorrow for coffee and talk more?"

"Sure, I suppose," he said.

"Actually, I was going to go by the townhouse today. Is that all right?" she asked and thought about the hypnosis papers in her desk. She wanted to get them to show to Bill.

"I have to go to work. Your dad has a project he wants to work on...some sort of proposal for the board. It's your stuff. Get it whenever you like." He shrugged.

"Good, thank you Henry."

"Kate, are you going to continue seeing him?" His eyes squinted down and he looked angry.

"Henry, that isn't important and, really, it's none of your business. Don't make me get ugly, okay?" Kate started to feel tired again and thought it would be a good idea to get a little more sleep. She'd only been out of the hospital for a week and still worked on getting her strength back. "Henry, I guess I'm not as energetic as I thought I was. I'll stop over at the house later today, but right now I'm going to lie down," she said as she moved out of the kitchen.

"Fine, let me know when you'll be there. I'll figure out a way to leave work and meet you," he said and watched her back move away.

She turned around in the doorway. "You don't need to be there. I only need to pick up some papers and clothes. We'll talk more, later."

On her way up the stairs, she heard her grandmother call out to her. Kate opened the door and found her sitting in a chair by the window. Grammy put her needlepoint piece down on her lap when Kate entered the room.

"I saw you drive up late last night. Your mom and dad seemed a little worried. I bet there was hell to pay," Grammy said, and grinned like the Cheshire cat.

"Not too much. Dad knew where I was." Kate sat on the window ledge next to her chair.

Grammy picked her needlepoint back up and continued to stitch. "Your mother wasn't very happy."

"Grammy, do you remember Connor O'Leary?"

"Of course I remember him. He was... hmmm...how is it said these days? Oh yes, he was a yummy, hottie for our time." She giggled.

Kate couldn't believe what she'd just heard and laughed. "Grammy, I'm shocked that you would use such a phrase. Something really interesting happened yesterday."

"Oh, please, do tell, missy," Grammy said.

"I met a man who looks just like Connor. In fact, he knew the whole story about Connor and Lizzie."

"The whole story? It was no story, Lizzie dear. It really happened and you shouldn't act all surprised. You lived it, for Pete's sake." Grammy put her needlepoint down in her lap and looked seriously at Kate. "Why are you here, Liz? You should be setting up your new household with your husband, not dallying around the family home."

Kate sat up straight and stared at her grandmother. She leaned over and put her hand on her grandmother's arm. "Ground control to Grammy, this is Kate." Kate looked at her hopefully.

"I know who you are," she said and frowned at her granddaughter. "I was surprised that Effie didn't show up, though. She was so jealous of you and Connor. Wherever you two went, she followed. It made her crazy in the head the amount of time you two spent together." She squeezed her eyes shut. "Lizzie, I think I need one of my tablets."

Kate moved into her bathroom and found the bottle of nitroglycerin tablets. She quickly returned to the room and placed the tablet under her grandmother's tongue. "Is that helping, Grammy?"

Her grandmother opened her eyes and gazed at Kate with a bit of a smile. She finally shook her head and said, "I'm okay. It just seems I get confused more than usual. I called you Lizzie, didn't I?"

"Yeah, you did." Kate moved a footstool and sat down in front of her. "Grammy, I know you don't like to talk about what happened, but tell me about Connor and Elizabeth?"

Kate's grandmother frowned deeper. "Elizabeth was my older sister, you know?" Kate nodded her head yes. "It's hard to talk about. It was so sad. They were so in love. When Connor first came to town, I remember people talking about the young Irish fellow who took over the stable. One day, when we were walking to school, we saw him. He was so handsome." She stopped and looked away from Kate. "He was kind and always brought me treats from the mercantile. Maybe I am getting senile. I remember it like it was yesterday."

"No, Grammy, it's not possible you're going senile." Her grandmother turned her gaze back to Kate. "I met this man, his name is Bill Leary. He works as a teacher at the community college and a mechanic in an auto shop."

"Leary is his last name, not O'Leary? Is he related to Connor?"

"Yeah, he is. His grandfather was related to Connor. We have some more research to do, but that's what Bill found out."

Grammy shook her head. "Does he look very much like Connor?"

"Yeah, almost exactly like, except Bill's hair is a little lighter. Grammy, how did they meet?"

"Lizzie was about eighteen years old when they meet. I can't remember how old Connor was, maybe twenty-six or twenty-seven. She was teaching at the school. We always walked down the street past the stables to go to school and for awhile they just exchanged glances. Lizzie was ten years older than me so I was only about eight at the time, but I could tell. I could see the looks they gave each other. Lizzie got up the nerve one day to talk to him. She invited him to a social for the following Sunday after church services. He courted her for about two years before he asked our father for permission to marry her. She was so lovely on their wedding day," Grammy grew quiet. "It was so terrible what happened."

"They died in the hotel fire?" Kate asked.

"Yes." She took her granddaughter's hand and squeezed it. "I was young and my memory is not real clear anymore. I think I remember..."

The door to her grandmother's room swung open and her mom entered. "I thought you were going to get some rest?"

"Listening in on my brief conversation with Henry, Mom? We were just chatting." Kate squeezed her grandmother's hand and got up. "We'll talk later, okay Grammy?"

Kate walked out and headed for her own room. Her mom followed her down the hall. "Kate, you really need to take it easy. All of this running around isn't good for you right now. Please, don't push yourself too hard, okay?"

Kate turned to face her. "Mom, I'm doing fine. I did push myself a little too much yesterday, but I won't make any progress if I'm treated like a baby." Kate opened the door and entered her bedroom. She kicked off her shoes, turned and sat on the bed. Her mom stood in the doorway with her arms crossed. "What, Mom?"

"I'm just worried that's all, I..." She didn't continue.

"Mom, I know everything that's happened over the last couple of weeks upsets you, but right now I really need for you to let me get back on my feet. If I'm going to get my bearings back, I need room." Kate looked at her mother and hoped she'd gotten through. "Besides, I know you have other things you'd rather be doing than nursing me and I am getting better. You said you had to go into work. That should help take your mind off of me." Kate lay back onto the bed and then propped herself up on her elbows. "By the way, I won't be home for dinner tonight."

"Are you meeting Henry for dinner?" her mom asked and tried to sound cheerful.

"No, I'm meeting Henry at the house this afternoon. I need to start packing up some things." Kate lay back again and adjusted the pillow under her head.

"Who, then?"

"The new friend I told you about."

"The mechanic?" Maggie asked and shook her head. "I just don't want you to overdo it again today. Don't stay out too late, all right?" Her mom turned to leave Kate's room. "Sweetheart, you shouldn't give up on Henry so quickly. He cares for you."

There was that care word again. Kate raised her hand and cut her off. "Mom, I'm really tired now and I'm going to get some rest. We can discuss this later."

Her mom looked a bit hurt, but agreed Kate needed her rest and left the room. Kate wanted to think about Bill Leary and what all this could possibly mean, but suddenly felt tired and fell to sleep.

For the first time in ages, she had a regular dream - or so she thought. She heard voices in her sleep. The one she heard the most was Connor's voice telling her about the life that they had to look forward to. She remembered this moment so well. They were out in a field of summer wildflowers and grasses. He'd gotten down on one knee and held her hand between his. He wanted to speak to her father and he would be most honored if she would accept his proposal of marriage. She remembered barely being able to speak; she was so taken with all Connor said to her. When she accepted him, tears rolled down her cheeks and, as she looked at him could tell he was choked up, too. He had given her a wonderful, tender kiss that day and she realized she'd never forget this one moment.

71

Then, something changed. Everything around her went dark and a voice screamed at her that she could never be with another man. She was his and she saw Henry standing at the edge of the field, but it wasn't Henry. It was someone she didn't recognize and for some reason she was frightened by him.

Kate awoke and sat up on her bed. She sucked in her breath and tried hard not to scream. After a few minutes, she calmed down, but couldn't remember why she was so scared. There was something wrong with the dream that gnawed at her insides. Connor hadn't proposed to Lizzie in a field. If she remembered correctly, he proposed on the front porch of Lizzie's parents' house.

Chapter Ten

After she rested most of the morning, Kate woke up. She lay on her bed and thought about this new version of a dream she'd had before. She felt it could be some sort of guilt that spilled over into her sleep. She didn't know what to think.

She reached to the end of the bed, grabbed her purse and pulled out her book from the hospital. She found the number for the people who did regression hypnosis that the psychiatrist had given her.

She pulled her cell phone out and dialed the number. After she listened to a message and waited for the beep, she ran through her mind what she wanted to say. Then the beep came and she started. "Hi, my name is Kate Sullivan and I'd like to arrange a meeting with you, ah, to discuss dreams. My cell phone number is 555-0361. You can reach me anytime. Okay, thank you." As she clicked off her phone, she mumbled to herself, "I hate answering machines." She rolled off the bed and put on her shoes.

Whether her mom was still around or not Kate wasn't sure. She managed to leave the house quietly. Kate made her way back to the townhouse she'd shared with Henry and let herself in. She'd already stopped at an Office Depot on the way there and picked up cardboard boxes to fill.

She looked around the living room and it brought back many memories, some good, some not so good. She went into the extra bedroom they used as an office. Sitting down at her desk, she started to dig through the drawers.

Sometime ago she put the dream information into a manila folder, but it wasn't in the file drawer. She opened the middle drawer and found the folder she'd sought. She flipped through the contents, and felt like it was the first time she'd seen any of this. Kate stuck the folder into her purse. She leaned back in her chair and thought about packing up some of her clothing, but then glanced at the bookshelf and saw a couple of the books on dreams she had purchased. She got up, retrieved the books, and added them to a box.

She started to empty her desk. In one of the drawers she found pictures of her and Henry. She put another box together for old boyfriend stuff and threw in the pictures. It wasn't something she wanted to go through right now.

She was about halfway finished with her desk when she heard the front door open and footsteps on the stairs. She turned and watched the doorway as the steps continued down the hall. When Henry turned into the room, Kate let out a breath. "Jeez, Henry, are you trying to give me a heart attack?"

"Yeah, I was," he said and stared at her.

Kate frowned at him. "I was joking."

"I wasn't," he said and turned down the hall to the master bedroom.

She heard him change his clothes, knowing the sound of his shoes being slammed against the back of the closet. She thought this might be a good time to leave.

Henry reappeared in ripped jeans and a T-shirt. He stood in the doorway and leaned against the jamb. "We're supposed to be going to the Taylor's for a Halloween party in a couple of weeks. I don't suppose you're going to want to do that?" he asked.

"You know I've always thought Halloween was a highly over-rated holiday." She tried to smile, but found it difficult.

"I'll let them know we won't be attending, then." Henry looked at her. "Kate, I'm not ready to give us up. I know you need some time to think things over and that's fine. I'll be here waiting for you to come back."

"I would be lying to you if I said there was a chance. What I said at my parents last night and this morning still holds. We've grown too far apart."

"I don't understand, how have we grown apart?"

"Henry, we're going in different directions. I'm finding other interests you don't find all that interesting. I want to settle down and maybe have a family, and you don't."

He nodded. "Other interests, right. This wouldn't have anything to do with the garage jerk you visited last night?"

Kate looked at him curiously. "What is that supposed to mean?"

"Your mom said you have dinner plans this evening. Pretty quick seeing as you just met him yesterday," he said with a sarcastic tone of voice.

"Mom said? You two have been talking? Now, that's very interesting." Kate stood up, picked up her purse and set her car keys on top of a box. She picked it up by the handles and started toward the door. Henry straightened up and stood in her way.

"Excuse me, please," she said and looked at him over the box.

"You know why I followed you last night? I wanted to make sure you were safe. I saw you go to the grease monkey's house. You never did answer me. Did he fuck you?" Henry sneered.

"Henry, please, let's not do this. Get out of my way," Kate said and moved forward with the box. She tried to push him out of the way.

"Let's do what, Kate?"

"Play adolescent games. I need to leave anyway."

Henry snickered. "That's right, we're both grownups aren't we? I can't believe you're sleeping with a mechanic. Is he really dirty with you?"

"I'm not doing this. Please get out of my way," she growled and moved hard with the box which caused Henry to take a step back.

He put his arm against the wall and blocked her again. "I still hate you for laughing at me," he said.

"When did I laugh at you? When? I've never laughed at you, not once," she said and moved around him. She took quick steps and hurried to the stairs.

"Interesting you accuse me of selective memory. You don't even remember," he whispered.

"I have no idea what you're talking about. I've never laughed at you." She stopped at the top and turned around. "Henry, this is all obviously too complex for you. When you decide to act normal again, call me and we can talk."

"Too complex? How's that? You just meet a guy and you're already fucking him. How could it already be too complex?" Henry's voice rose.

"Henry, your jealous side was never very attractive and it isn't now. I have nothing to explain to you," Kate said and looked him in the eye. Her cell phone began to ring in her purse. She pulled it out and hit the answer button, "Hello?"

"Hey, I just wondered how soon we could get together. I've been thinking about you," Bill said.

Kate closed her eyes and tried to not grin. "I'm just leaving the townhouse. I'll see you soon."

"Good. Drive carefully, okay?"

"That sounds fine; I'll be about half an hour. Ok, bye." She turned the phone off and held it to her lips. "I'll be moving my stuff out in the next couple of weeks. I'll leave a message for you at the office and let you know when." Kate turned and started down the stairs.

Henry followed her down. "This isn't over, Kate. I'm not going to say 'okay, you don't love me anymore, I give up.' I'm not going to do that. I still love you and I know we can work this out."

Kate turned back to look at him. "That's funny, Henry. We've been together for five years and that's the first time in at least a year you've said 'I love you.' Isn't that odd?" She walked out of the townhouse. She felt she hadn't handled the discussion very well. *How do you tell someone that the relationship is over and get it through their stubborn brain*, she wondered?

Continuing out to her car, she put the box on the passenger seat and closed the door. She turned and headed for the driver side looking at Henry. "I'll be here next Saturday to finish packing and moving my furniture out."

He moved fast and pushed her hard against the side of her car. He held her upper arms very tightly. Kate hit her head on the window frame and saw stars.

"I don't think you heard me, Lizzie. I'm not going to lose you again," he whispered in her ear. "Maybe I should chain you up in the basement like we've seen in those thriller movies. If I do that maybe you'll consider staying," he said almost as an afterthought. He started to slide a hand up her waist.

She quickly tried to clear her brain. She squinted at him. "Henry, let me go and we'll pretend this didn't happen. Why did you call me Lizzie?"

He started to laugh. "No," he said and slammed her against the car once more. "I'm not letting that jerk touch you...ever! You're mine. Don't you see that we're destined to be together?"

Kate closed her eyes and sighed. "I didn't want to do this, but you leave me no choice." She brought her good leg up quickly, into his groin.

Henry shouted, and let go of her arms. He fell to the ground, grabbed his crotch with both hands, squeezed his eyes shut tight and groaned.

Kate turned fast and sat down in her car. She locked the doors and jammed the key into the ignition, then sped out of the parking lot onto the road.

When she was about a mile away, she pulled the VW over to the side of the road and turned it off. She put her elbows on the steering wheel, and tried to keep from sobbing. She didn't want to cry over Henry anymore, but his actions had hurt not only physically, it hurt her heart, too. She sat back in the seat and tried to make sense of his actions. Sure, he was hurt about their break up, but he'd never acted this way before. She couldn't figure out what he'd meant about not losing her again and chaining her in the basement. They didn't even *have* a basement. She also wondered why he called her Lizzie. That made no sense to her at all. She'd never told him the story of her dreams. Maybe her mother said something to him or he'd overheard her and Dad talk about the dreams.

She rubbed her upper arms and could feel sore spots. She pulled up the sleeve on her shirt and could see red splotch marks on her arms. When she got back to her parents' house, she'd put on a long-sleeved pullover sweater. She didn't want Bill to see her arms.

In the five years they'd been together, Henry never hurt her. He did develop one problem that made Kate furious though. He began to drink heavily on a regular basis. Sometimes he'd have one or two drinks, but at other times, more. He'd fall asleep the minute he got into bed and sometime wake up with dreadful headaches. Kate tried to discuss the situation with him, but he thought she overreacted and didn't want to talk about it.

It all came to a head over the Labor Day weekend. They were invited to a friend's house for a barbecue on Saturday.

Kate decided it was a good time to look for a separate apartment and end the relationship. She'd resolved in her mind to tell Henry of her plans first thing Sunday morning. Just one more party to attend as a couple and then it would end. She felt comfortable with her decision and knew it was the best she could do.

It was around three in the afternoon when they arrived at the barbecue and Henry began to drink. Kate tried to get him to eat, but he said he wasn't hungry. By ten in the evening, Kate decided it was time to go. She made excuses and joked that they needed to get up early for church in the morning. Kate tried gracefully to leave. Henry wouldn't give her the car keys and insisted he could drive. She knew she shouldn't get in. She knew she should take a cab or ask one of her friends to help out.

Kate stayed silent and got into the car. She knew Henry could tell she was mad and he decided to have some fun. He sped up and then slowed down. He ran several red lights. Secretly, Kate hoped a state trooper would see this and pull him over. But it that didn't happen. Henry began to weave down the highway and laughed and whooped. He'd look over at her with a big grin on his face to see if she was scared. She just stared at him. They never saw the SUV come toward them. Suddenly, she saw a bright light out of the corner of her eye. When she looked ahead, it was too late.

Of the four high school boys in the SUV two survived and two died. The van's gas tank leaked and a spark started a fire. The driver's blood alcohol level was higher than Henry's, which Kate thought was impossible. The SUV crossed over into their lane and hit them head-on at fifty miles per hour.

Because Henry was drunk, he did get a DUI, but since the boys were drunker, Henry didn't get blamed for the accident. Kate hit her head on the windshield and had a concussion. Her hip separated. Henry didn't have a scratch on him, but according to her mom, he felt very guilty. The first week of September didn't really exist for her. The day after the accident she was stable enough for the doctors to do surgery and fix her hip.

***

Bill called her while she was at the townhouse. He said he was at his house and working in the yard. She drove back to his place in Highwood. When she pulled into his driveway, he came around the side of the garage to greet her.

"Hey," he said and smiled, but it faltered. "What's the matter?"

She got out of the car and walked up to him. "Hello. There's nothing in the world wrong. Why?"

He leaned over to give her a kiss and put his hands on her waist. "You look like you've been crying." He reached around her and started to give her a hug, but she jerked and took a step back.

Kate didn't realize her back was so sore. She felt tight across the shoulders and found herself push away from him.

"Hey, what's the matter with your back?" He frowned and held onto her hand. "Kate, what happened?"

"Nothing, I just over-did the packing thing today," she said and tried to move past him into the house.

Bill turned with her and continued to hold her hand as they crossed into the front entrance.

She pulled her hand to remove it from his grip. "Bill, let go please."

He did let her hand go, but as she moved away from him he grabbed hold of the top of her pants. "Kate, why are you lying to me?" He refused to let her move away.

She looked up at him over her shoulder. "He was quite cruel to her," she said in a voice not quite her own.

"What?" Bill looked at her and put his hand on her arm, which caused her to cringe. "Kate, take your sweater off." He continued to stare at her.

"No," she said.

He still held onto the back of her pants, and his free hand began to tug the back of her sweater up to her shoulder.

"Bill, stop it." She pulled it back down.

"Let me see, please." He tightened his grip on her pants.

She looked up at him. It made her angry that he tried to tell her what to do, but he did say 'please.' "Okay, fine." She moved her sweater up to her shoulders and then pulled it all the way off. She saw the look on Bills face change when he viewed her back and the black and blue rings around her upper arms. Henry had grabbed her hard but she didn't think there would be bruises.

Bill lightly touched her arms and looked at her shoulder. "We should get some ice on this one, you've got a very purple lump," he said, quietly and lightly touched her skin.

He let go of her pants and went into the kitchen. She heard the refrigerator open and something, which could only be an ice tray crunch. She heard other noises and wasn't sure what he was doing.

"What did you mean?" he asked, as he came out of the kitchen. He held a plastic baggie with the ice cubes and a towel around it.

"About what?" Kate said, as she put her sweater back on.

"You said he was quite cruel to her." Bill put the ice on her shoulder blade.

Kate frowned and didn't know what he was talking about. "I don't remember saying that."

"So, are you going to tell me what happened?"

81

"Tell you what? That Henry showed up while I was packing boxes and acted like an ass? I didn't want to wreck a perfectly decent evening," she said.

Bill held onto the ice bag. "I may have to beat him to a pulp."

"See, that is exactly why I wasn't going to say anything. I didn't know how you'd react. Now, I know." She shook her head and moved past him toward the front door. She picked up her purse and pulled her keys out.

"Kate, wait...just wait," Bill said, as he followed her to the door. He put his hand on the knob and blocked her from opening it.

"Look Bill, I don't believe in beating the snot out of people just for revenge. It's stupid. He did it. The bruises will go away. I'll know better than to be left alone with him now." She tried to move him away from the door.

"Has he ever done this before?"

"Never. It was weird. He wasn't himself, obviously."

Bill reached over her shoulder and put the bag of ice on her back. She felt him pull her close and lean against the door. She moved her hands to his waist and wrapped her arms around him.

"Bill, if it helps any at all, I did kick him in the balls," she said, and glanced up at him.

"What?" He looked down at her.

"Let me rephrase that. I gave him a knee to the groin and left him in a crumpled ball on the driveway." She glanced up again, and looked into his blue eyes.

"I see. I guess that's even better than beating the pulp out of him." He leaned down and kissed her nose. "Don't leave."

"I'm not sure where I thought I was going. I really don't want to see my mom right now. I've got to find my own place next week."

He turned her around and they went into his living room. "I'm fixing dinner. We'll eat some fairly good food and talk. How does that work for you?" he asked.

"Fine, something *does* smell good," she said and sat down on his couch.

She saw him look down at her and it was obvious he was trying not to laugh. "Kate, did you really knee Henry in the balls? Now, I think I know how you'd react if you were mad at me and I tried to stop you from leaving."

She tilted her head to the side as her lips started to curl at the ends. "Yeah, I suppose it's a dead giveaway."

He handed her the ice bag. "I'm making a meatloaf and I hope it comes out all right. Wait here a minute. I have to mash the potatoes. I'll be right back. Do you want anything to drink?" he asked as he walked into the kitchen.

"No ... yes. Coffee if you have it," she said.

Chapter Eleven

Bill made a nice dinner. Kate felt impressed that Bill seemed to know his way around the kitchen. She helped him clean up afterward and then they sat on the couch having a dessert of cookies and coffee.

"You know, it's weird, but one time I was in West Seattle and had the hardest time finding my way around. I tried to find the old places, but couldn't figure it out. Do you know if Connor and Lizzie were buried over there?" Bill asked.

"Yeah, they are. I went over with my mom and dad a last year for Aunt Delia's funeral and saw the graves. My grandmother married and raised my dad and his brothers over there," Kate said.

"There's a beach somewhere...Lord, I can't seem to remember names tonight," he began.

"Alki Point. There's a park called Jefferson that I don't think was named when Lizzie and Connor walked it." Kate said. "The MacDiarmid's, and the Sullivan's lived just off of California Avenue. I guess you must have known the MacDiarmid's. Anyway, my dad was born and raised over there. We could drive over sometime. See if we could nail down locations. It would be interesting to see if the stable and school are still standing. It's doubtful I suppose, but it wouldn't hurt. There's a park over there that I've been to, for bird-watching. If the weather's nice we could get some food and have a picnic."

"You like bird-watching?" he asked.

"Definitely amateur stuff. I've been all over Washington State and Canada with a bird group, just to see if we can spot some particular species. I'm an amateur though. There are too many variations on a theme in the bird world. It's hard to remember them all."

Bill pressed his lips together. "I've done some bird-watching, too, in the eastern part of the state. Turkey vultures are great fun, but I have to agree. There are too many varieties to keep track of. It's funny, but I don't think Connor was into bird-watching."

Kate laughed. "Elizabeth, neither." She looked across the couch and then out the window. "What are you doing tomorrow?"

"I have nothing planned."

"How would you feel about a drive over to West Seattle? I think I can find where Connor and Lizzie are buried. I'd like to visit the grave for some reason, I can't begin to explain. We could put some flowers down for them." She smiled.

"I'd like that."

"Bill, let's get serious here a minute. How do you really feel about hypnosis?"

"It could be a little scary, I suppose. Why?"

She stood up and walked over to her purse, pulled out the folder of articles and brought it back to the couch, then handed it to him. "Here's something to help you sleep tonight. Regression hypnosis seems to be the treatment of choice. It does make me a bit nervous, though."

"Why?" he asked.

"I guess I've seen too many movies and read too much about it. I have a fear of becoming like one of those spiritualists that channel the two-thousand-year-old ghost of some medicine man. If we were to do hypnosis what if we start channeling some strange prophet who tells us we need to meditate more and do yoga?" She started to laugh and sat back beside him.

"And tells us we were abused by our parents in 1507," he continued.

"I know it sounds silly to be afraid, but I don't know. It's not really a scientifically-grounded, FDA approved form of treatment. I know. I'm acting weird."

"No, you're not weird, or crazy...well, maybe just a little. I don't think it would be unusual for us to feel just a little bit weary. I've never experienced hypnosis and, from what you've said, I don't think you have either. I looked up some stuff on the Internet this afternoon and you're right. Some of the information said that when you have a dream you remember, you should write it down the minute you wake up. Did you ever do that?" He looked hopefully at Kate.

"No. I've never written anything down." She finished her coffee and set the cup on the table in front of her. "While I was still in the hospital, I met with a psychiatrist. He gave me the names of a couple in Everett who practice hypnosis. I did leave a message for the Sheridans this afternoon. Come to think of it, I'm not really very good at leaving voice messages and I didn't give much information. I think I'll see if they have an email address and maybe send them a synopsis of our story. We probably won't hear anything right away, but who knows? Maybe they'll be interested. What is your class schedule?"

"My first class Monday thru Friday is at 8:00 a.m. to 10:00 a.m. On Wednesday I have an afternoon class," Bill said and leaned closer to her. "There is supposed to be a staff lunch on Friday, but I could probably get out of that."

"I doubt we'll hear from them by then. Go to the lunch." She picked up her coffee and looked at the bottom of the cup.

"Do you want some more coffee?" he asked, and reached for her empty cup.

"Bill, we've known each other for twenty-four hours now. Do you feel a little strange being able to sit and discuss things so comfortably?"

His hand dropped and she saw his brows come together. She thought he might find it a difficult question to answer.

"No. I don't think I feel weird. We sort of know each other's history." He glanced at her. "Even though we just met, we have a common ground which makes discussing things with you very easy. Does that make sense?"

"Yeah, I believe you've hit the nail on the head." She smiled. "I had a regular dream this morning."

"What?"

"I think it was a regular dream. It was out of context." She saw him frown. "The dreams always run in order, from the beginning to the end. This one wasn't in order." She set the empty cup down and turned to him. "In fact, it wasn't really how I remember this happening. Do you remember when Connor asked Lizzie to marry him?"

"Sure, they were sitting on her parents' porch. He got down on one knee and asked her. Then he went into the house and asked Mr. MacDiarmid's permission."

"Right, that's right. I remember it that way, too. In my dream this morning, they were sitting in a huge field of wildflowers and green grass. The colors were so vibrant. Lizzie cried when she said yes. For some reason, Henry was standing on the edge of the field, shouting something. I can't remember what it was, but I woke up really scared. I don't know, I suppose everything could have caught up with me and spilled over into my subconscious."

"How do you feel about it now?" He took her hand and kissed the back of it.

"Fine. It's been a crazy day." Kate smiled and liked that they continued to discuss their own childhoods and schooling, where they'd gone, when they'd finished. They talked about movies and books they found of interest.

When they turned back to the topic that brought them together and started to compare memories from the dream,

Kate was so relaxed and calm. They talked about things that hadn't been in the dream, but that they knew was a part of it. The conversation lasted until well after midnight.

Bill walked her out to her car. He got a quizzical look on his face and asked, "Do you remember once when we walked down to the shoreline line together and you found a particular shell?"

Kate suddenly felt uneasy and backed away from him. "You said 'we.'"

He looked at her and leaned against her car, then looked at the pavement and said, "You're right. I did say 'we.'" He shook his head and ran his hand through his hair. "Let me ask you this. Are you still having problems figuring out if the feelings you might have for me are yours or Lizzie's?"

"I hadn't really thought about it, but it is a valid point." Kate leaned against the car, too. "I know I had a particularly tough time when I woke up after the accident. Past and present ran headlong into one another. I'm not sure where the feelings are coming from. Bill, do you believe in reincarnation? I mean do you think it might be a possibility?"

"I've done a little reading about it, but never thought it possible. Right now, though, when I look at you, I suppose anything could be possible. I know, for a fact, that this whole evening, as I sat on the couch next to you, it was all I could do to keep my hands off of you. Then I thought, what if this feeling isn't mine? Once, I would have thought reincarnation unlikely, but now that we're talking about it, I'd have to say it's a door we shouldn't shut just yet. Agreed?" he asked.

"I agree and I had the same problem on the couch." They were silent for a minute. She finally looked up at him and grinned. "Do you remember the week before the wedding?"

"Yes, I do."

"Do you remember the barn?"

Bill smiled and arched a brow. "Miss Sullivan, you aren't referring to that night of hot, passion, three days before the legal ceremony, are you?"

"When I had that dream, I was completely blown away. I spent the better part of a week trying to figure out what it meant and nearly drove myself nuts. To be honest, I wanted that one to repeat. It was hot."

"It was interesting, particularly the part with the horses that stood around, chomped their oats and watched. What do you think now?"

Kate laughed. "I'm not sure what to think and it is late."

Bill looked at his watch. "Yeah, we both need to get some sleep." He smiled at her, said goodnight, gave her a quick kiss and started to walk away. He stopped and turned around. "Say, one thing. Are you doing anything for New Years Eve?"

She stood at her open car door and smiled. "Nothing comes to mind. I'm usually in bed by ten o'clock on New Years. I've never been a very big fan."

"Neither am I, but, how would you feel about doing the Space Needle thing, just this year? We need to celebrate our meeting. I saw it once when I was a teenager and have always been curious to see the fireworks go off again. There's a hotel down near the Needle and its early enough, maybe we could get a reservation and watch from a room. That way we could have champagne safely and not have to hassle with the downtown traffic. "

"I don't suppose it would hurt anything. It is still a couple of months away. I just hope I can stay awake. I'll have to take a nap in the afternoon." Kate smiled. "What were you going to say about walking by the shore and finding a shell?"

"I just remember *Connor* and *Elizabeth* walking by the shore a lot." He made a point of accentuating their names. "I wonder what ever happened to that shell."

"I see. You know, we could probably keep talking all night. I'd better go."

***

They said goodnight. This time, Bill waited until she got in the car and watched her drive off. He walked back to his house, unsure of what he felt for her. It bothered him that he had said 'we' when referring to Connor and Elizabeth. In a way, though, it didn't bother him.

He locked the front door and went into the living room. He looked at the couch and smiled. He thought about how beautiful she looked when she thought about their situation and made comments.

He picked up the coffee cups and took them into his kitchen. His cell phone was on the table and it started to buzz. He scooped it up and saw it was Kate.

"Hello, darling woman." He grinned.

"Hi. I just realized I didn't thank you for a great dinner. It was very good and I admire your kitchen skills." She sounded as though she was smiling.

"I'll have to show you what I can do with a blender sometime." He leaned against the counter. "I'm honored that you admire me."

"I do, you know - admire you. I know it's only been two days, but we are making plans for New Years and I have a lot of hope...I don't know. I'm just being weird again."

He smiled. "I don't think you're weird. I was wondering...since we've already made plans for the New Year, and you don't have to answer me now, but do you have any plans for Thanksgiving and Christmas?" He heard the line go silent. "See, I haven't cooked a turkey ever and I want to try it. I'd also like to get a tree this year and know I'm going to need help getting it decorated." He listened to her breathe on the other end of the line.

"I'd love it," she answered.

"You don't have to say *yes* now; I just wanted to put the invite out there."

"I don't need to think about it, Bill. I'd really love to spend the holidays with you."

"Great. It's a date." He pumped his fist. "Kate, drive carefully."

"I will. Goodnight."

"Goodnight." He clicked the phone off and held it to his lips. "I'm going to have good dreams again tonight."

***

When Kate got home, everyone appeared to be asleep. She went to her bedroom and turned her computer on. After she brushed her teeth, she put on her pajama's and sat down in front of the screen. She opened up the Internet and found that the Sheridans did have a website. She found a *contact us* connect and hit it. She spent the next hour and a half composing an email to the Sheridans explaining her and Bill's story. When she finally hit the send button it was after three in the morning and she was tired. She crawled into bed and pulled the quilt up to her neck. She could hear Bill's voice asking her over for the holidays and grinned ear to ear.

Chapter Twelve

A fine drizzle fell all morning in Seattle the next day. Kate met Bill at his house and they headed south on I-5 by ten o'clock.

"It's really strange, but I feel apprehensive about seeing the grave," Kate said, and looked out the truck window.

Bill reached up to the dashboard and turned on the wipers and then patted her hand. "Why is that?"

"I don't know. I just feel weird." She shook her head.

He put his hand on top of hers, and gave her a light squeeze. "It will be okay. How old was Delia when she passed? Did you know her very well?"

"I'm not sure how old she was. She came to family gatherings for holidays when I was a kid, but I never talked to her much. She and Grammy were close, so I know they saw a lot of each other."

"I remember Dee." He looked at Kate and realized she hadn't heard him.

"I saw the stone when I walked back to my car at Delia's funeral. It didn't really register until later when I got home. I've always meant to come back, but never got around to it. I just hope I can find it again." She fell silent.

Bill felt she was deep in thought about something and didn't ask any more questions. He watched the road, made his way carefully through Seattle and followed the signs to the West Seattle Bridge.

He watched the weather and was glad they'd decided to wear coats and not pack a picnic lunch. It was a chilly, gray day in the city. As they crossed the bridge, Kate read the directions they'd gotten from the Internet out loud to Bill. After a couple of wrong turns, they found the right street and soon the green lawn appeared on the left side of the truck.

Bill felt her grab onto his hand and, when he looked at her, realized her eyes welled up with tears. "Kate, are you okay?" he asked.

She was staring at the cemetery. "Yeah, it's just sad."

There was a big sign, Forrest Green Cemetery, over the driveway into the graveyard. Bill turned left and followed the road around a couple of turns until Kate said to stop. He found a place to park and shut off the truck.

They sat in the warm truck for a few minutes and looked at the area around them. Kate glanced over at him and smiled. "No time like the present, right?"

He watched her open the door and slide out to the sidewalk, and then he helped her pull the seat forward and she grabbed a sack that held flowers. Bill heard her close her side and walked around the truck to meet her on the other side.

They followed a path with Kate leading the way. It took several minutes, but they finally found Delia's headstone. She was buried in the same area with her parents and others from the MacDiarmid clan.

Kate set the bag down, pulled out a bunch flowers, and laid them by the marker. She glanced up at Bill. "I remember Delia was furious at the number of buttons on the back of the wedding gown. She spent ten or fifteen minutes getting the thing done up. She even cursed Mother a couple of times."

"She gave me an earful the day before the wedding." Bill chuckled.

"About what?"

"It was all about how I needed to treat her sister with respect and kindness. She cornered me in the stable for about an hour. I was certain she was going to call in the reverend to lecture me, too. I thanked God she didn't know we'd already been together."

93

Kate walked up to him and put her arms around his waist. She rested her head on his chest. His hands wound around her back and held on tight.

"My sister was definitely ahead of her time. She would have made a fine suffragette by 1910."

Bill laughed. He felt warmth radiate from her. "You feel so good."

"I've missed you so much."

Bill nuzzled her neck. "My love, it has been a terrible long time without you." Bills voice suddenly had an Irish accent.

Kate pulled back and looked up at him as he put his hands on either side of her neck. He lowered his lips onto hers, lightly, and she responded, parting hers.

Warmth flowed between them and both felt as though they were floating. Their lips parted and Bill looked down into her warm blue eyes. He touched her cheek and kissed her again.

She pulled her head back and he watched her lick her lips. Then she gasped and took a step back. "Oh my, that was weird."

Bill didn't move his hands and smiled. "It was strange, yes, but that was a nice kiss."

She started to walk away from him. "I still think you're an excellent kisser," she said over her shoulder. "Lizzie and Connor are over this way." She leaned over to pick up the bag and then walked over to another row of graves.

He followed her to the next row and found himself taken by just watching her move. She moved from one gravesite to the next and made sure not to step on the graves themselves. He smiled and felt more for her than he thought possible. He thought it remarkable that she actually respected the memories of those buried around them.

Under a tall cedar tree, they found the marker. *Elizabeth MacDiarmid O'Leary born August 8, 1892 and Connor James O'Leary born May 3, 1885, both perished June 23, 1912 The Lord took them too soon.*

He watched as Kate touched the headstone and traced the letters with her fingers. The granite looked cold and wet from the drizzle. She took the flowers out of the bag and placed them next to the stone. He didn't realize it, but she'd started to cry. Tears rolled down her cheeks.

Bill looked around the grounds. "You know, I think this is where that barn used to be. There's the church over on the other side of the cemetery. I remember there was a smaller cemetery on the other side of the drive, but this side used to be a farm. I think that's right."

When he heard her blow her nose, he looked down and saw Kate had taken a tissue out of her pocket. She wiped her eyes and stared at the stone. Memories flooded through his brain and he wanted to know what she felt, but was afraid to ask.

"We used to walk up that road over there. Your parents' house should be right around the corner," he said. He looked the other way and pointed. "My stable and foundry should be at the end of that road, with the school just a little farther down." He didn't realize his accent had changed again. "It's changed."

He turned back to Kate and saw she was down on her knees in the wet grass. She held her sides and rocked back and forth. He realized she was crying very hard, silently, and his heart broke. He walked over to her, squatted down beside her and put his arms around her shoulders.

"My love, don't be cryin'. It's all going to be made right, I promise."

She leaned against him and he sensed she tried to get her emotions under control. "It was so horrible, what happened that day." She looked up at him. "But it was a beautiful day, too. You were so handsome in your suit. I don't understand why any of it happened. Why did it have to be that one day?"

"I'm hopin' we'll get some answers, my lass."

The heavens opened up and the rain started coming down hard. They both stood up and ran back to the truck. They sat in the cab and Bill started the engine to turn on the heater. He reached behind his seat and pulled out a roll of paper towels.

"Why do you have paper towels in your truck, Bill?"

"They always come in handy. Sometimes the windows get fogged and if I'm not being particularly patient with the defroster, I can wipe them off." He smiled at her.

He and Kate dried off as best they could. Kate blew her nose again. He hoped she wouldn't cry anymore for awhile.

"I'm starting to feel like I have a split personality," she said.

He held a paper bag up for her to throw the towels into. He looked at her eyes and felt himself melt. "I knew coming here would be emotional, but I remember so many things."

Kate put her head in her hands. "I know they're not my memories, but they seem so normal and I don't know what to do with them. I don't know what I expected to accomplish today." He saw her shake her head and wipe her eyes again. She put the heels of her hands over her eyes. "And, it's really nice to have someone to talk to who doesn't think I'm crazy." He heard her sob again.

Bill scooted over in the seat, put his arms around her and held her tight. "Kate, sweetheart, I know exactly where you're coming from. One minute I think, 'I've known this lady for a couple of days' and then it's, 'I've known this lady for over one hundred years, we're married and I love her more than anything.'"

She put her hands on his arm and laughed. "What a pair we are, neither knowing if we're coming or going."

"We'll take it a day at a time. We won't do anything unless we both agree. Deal?"

She patted his arm and nodded. "Deal."

"Do you want to go find the house? I'm interested to see if the stable is still there," he said.

"I don't think horses have been in this area for a while, Bill. We can look, though."

He moved back to his seat, and put the truck into Drive. They went up and down several streets and finally found the old MacDiarmid homestead.

"I think my Great-Aunt Delia lived there with her family and then it was sold. I'm not sure when, but a non-related family took it over. It hasn't changed too much, except for a new chimney and some paint," Kate said, as she looked out the truck window.

Bill felt good now that they knew where the house was located, it made finding the road to the stables and schoolhouse easier to find. It was paved now and much smoother than he remembered. When they found the lot where the stable had stood, he couldn't find any words to say. He looked at a strip mall. There was a dry-cleaners and a small Teriyaki Spot, but the rest of the building was for lease. He felt a little depressed by all the changes. The schoolhouse was completely gone and had become a parking lot.

"Maybe coming to West Seattle wasn't such a good idea," Kate said. "It's so different."

Bill pulled the truck into the center lane and speeded up. "Thomas Wolfe said 'you can't go home again.' I guess he hit that nail on the head."

On the freeway back to Seattle, he still couldn't find any words. Kate was quiet, too, and he heard her sniff and blow her nose a couple more times. He thought about what they'd seen. It was a surprise, but he was glad they went to West Seattle and felt it was something they'd needed to do.

"Have lunch with me, and dinner tonight. We could go to a movie or something." Bill smiled at Kate and reached for her hand.

She smiled at him and put her hand in his. "I think I'll skip the movie. I have to start looking for a place to live this next week and that can be exhausting."

***

Kate pulled her VW into the driveway at her parents' house around ten o'clock. She saw a shadow by her mother's car and recognized it immediately. Henry waited for her in the dark.

She got out of her car and slammed the door shut loud enough she hoped, for her parents to hear. As she looked at him, she thought she didn't even know him anymore. They hadn't had any kind of serious discussion in so long, she didn't know what to expect and she didn't like how it felt.

"What's going on Henry?" she asked, cautiously.

"Nothing. Where have you been all day? I've been looking for you."

"Why?"

"I think we should talk about us. I know I haven't been all that receptive to discuss where we're headed, but I think we need to get us sorted out, before we crash and burn." He started to move toward her.

"That's inappropriate phrasing, Henry. Crash and burn, really?" She shook her head and crossed her arms. "There's nothing I want to talk to you about anymore. We've been finished for a long time and I just didn't face it until recently. It became really clear yesterday when you slammed me against

98

the car. I don't love you, Henry. And, I think, you don't love me."

He stopped in his tracks and looked really surprised. "So now you know how I feel? When did you get psychic abilities?"

"Come on, if you really cared about us, we would have discussed it a couple of years ago. We both got too comfortable."

"What do you want then? How can I change your mind? What do I need to do?" He moved toward her and stood by her car.

Kate fell silent and thought about it. She didn't want anything he might offer. "It's too late, Henry. It's time we both moved on. You shouldn't have to change for anyone and neither should I. It seems like we both want different things and if you changed to make me happy you'd only end up hating me."

"No I wouldn't. I'd never hate you, Kate. I've loved you for so long. I need you in my life. I miss the warm spot you make in the bed next to me. It's been awfully cold since you left."

He tried to put his arm around her shoulders, but she side-stepped him and started to walk toward the house. Henry moved up behind her and spun her around. He pushed her against her mother's car. The outside light came on and she heard the front door open.

"Is that you, Kate?" She heard her mother's voice call.

"Yeah, Mom. I'll be right in." She looked up at Henry. "Let me go."

He smiled. "I just wanted a goodnight kiss." He started to lean toward her, but she turned her head. Henry looked angry, but released her arms and let her move away. "I know who you've been with. What does he have that's so great? Why do you keep going back to him?"

She walked up the path to the front steps where her mom stood in the light that came from the house. She turned and looked down at Henry. "I didn't think you had your license anymore. Why are you driving?" She saw him smirk at her and walk to his car.

"Is everything all right, Kate?" her mother asked as she walked into the house.

"Yeah, fine. I'm tired. Good night, Mom."

Chapter Thirteen

The week flew by quickly. Kate spent two days driving all over the map and tried to find an apartment. Finally at 4:30 p.m. on Wednesday she found not the home of her dreams, but a place she could live with for a while. It was in south Highwood about three blocks from where Bill lived. She laughed and thought he would label her as a stalker any day now.

The apartment turned out to be a one-bedroom, one-bath in the basement of a house. It was an older brick house and she could tell a lot of work was done to remodel it. The walls and window frames had been replaced and, except for the window in the door, all the others were two-pane thermal glass. The top half of the door had leaded, diamond shaped glass and was quite charming.

She'd been driving home from Bill's house when she saw the For Rent sign. The owners were an older couple. They only required a six-month lease and a small security deposit. The six months would fly by in no time. She filled out the application and the owner said after they did a credit check, they'd give her a call. Kate asked if all passed, would she be able to move in by the next weekend and one of the owners said she didn't think there would be a problem with that.

They asked her basic questions and she was honest with them and explained about the car accident a few months earlier and that she would go back to work by the end of the year. She told them about her job at the University and about her parents.

Her mother tried to get Kate to discuss the new friend she was seeing. After all the years her mom had treated the dream like an act of laziness, Kate decided it was best to keep quiet. She did tell her dad what was going on with Bill and why. He told her he didn't like the idea of hypnosis, and she tried to explain how serious she and Bill were to get questions about the dream answered once and for all. She watched her dad throw up his hands and he didn't argue with her. He did ask her that if anything further developed that he be kept in the loop, which she agreed to.

Kate also made arrangements with her dad to let her know when Henry was in the office. She went over to the townhouse on several short excursions and packed up what she could and stored several boxes in her parents' garage.

On Monday, of the following week, at about ten in the morning, Kate's cell phone rang. She sat in her parents' kitchen, drinking coffee and reading the newspaper. Fortunately, she was alone. She picked up the phone and hit the answer button.

"Hello?"

"Hello, could I speak to Kate Sullivan, please?" the voice asked.

"Yes, this is Kate," she answered.

"Hi. My name is Robin. I'm Jeff and Anna Sheridan's assistant. They received your email and are very interested in meeting with you. When can you come to the office?"

"Well, we could make it any day, except Wednesday. It would have to be in the afternoon, though."

"We?"

Kate silently chuckled to herself. *Here we go again with the we thing*, she thought. "Yes, there are two of us having the same dreams," Kate said. She hoped she didn't sound too weird. "The other person is Bill Leary. He wants to be involved, too."

"I see, well, how would tomorrow at two o'clock work?" Robin asked.

"I think that would work out fine. You can put us down. I'll check with Bill and if there's a schedule issue, I'll call back. Thank you."

"No problem, we'll see you tomorrow."

Kate clicked off her phone and set it on the table. This is going to be really strange, she thought to herself. She felt she needed to tell Bill. She looked at the clock above the stove, and saw it was after ten. She found his name on her cell phone and hit the dial button.

"Hey there," he answered. "What are you up to this fine morning?" She smiled at the sound of his voice.

"Not too much. I wanted to let you know I heard from the Sheridans this morning. They're very interested in our story. We have an appointment tomorrow at two o'clock. I just wanted to make sure you don't have anything on your agenda for that time?"

Bill was silent for a brief second. "Hmm, I'm so busy I just don't know how I'll be able to squeeze this in. Of course, I'll be free tomorrow," he said in a flip tone and started to laugh. "I don't think the students are feeling like they can ask me any questions this week."

"Funny. I'm so not busy I actually think going back to work sometime sooner than later would be a good thing. There's only so much daytime television to watch before brain rot sets in."

"So," Bill's voice said in her ear. "What are you doing for lunch? I'm having a terrible need for a greasy, cholesterol-infested hamburger."

Kate looked at her watch. "It's only 10:25. Are you really hungry?"

"Yes, starved."

"I did get up late this morning. I suppose I could get something light."

***

They ate a nice, quiet lunch at a small hamburger joint in Edmonds. They talked about the appointment, and wondered what it would be like. After they finished, Kate dropped Bill back at his office at the community college. He'd asked her if she wanted to have dinner that evening, but she said no. Kate felt she should eat with her parents and let them know about the apartment. She also wanted to fill her dad in on the latest news. Bill said he understood and it was probably best. He should prepare his class for the next day and had papers to grade.

As she drove back to her parents' house, she started to think about the appointment that she and Bill would attend the next day. Her stomach knotted up and began to feel a little sour. She said to herself, *I'm not going to get flaky about this, it's going to work out fine.* Neil Stein wouldn't have recommended the Sheridans if they weren't on the up and up. *Just keep thinking positive, Kate. It's going to be okay,* she thought. She pulled into her parents' driveway, turned off the car and walked into the house.

Her mom stood at the counter in the kitchen and prepared dinner. "Hey Mom," Kate said as she entered the room. She sat down at the table.

"Hey yourself," her mom said and stirred a pot on the stove.

"I found an apartment. I can move in right away. I'll finally be out of your hair."

Kate's mom turned from the stove and looked concerned, "An apartment? Are you sure you're ready? And, what about Henry?"

"Mom, you know Henry and I are no good right now. I know you like him, but he and I just aren't interested in the

104

same things anymore. He still thinks he's 18. He's got his issues that I do not want to live with and he doesn't think there is a problem, so..." She grew silent and looked out the back window.

Her mom came over to the table and sat across from Kate. "Honey, it doesn't matter if I like him or not. It matters that you like him and if you aren't happy then maybe it is time to move on. All I ask is that you don't throw away the time you and Henry were together. Relationships take hard work and if you're going to make this one survive, you have to put in the time. His behavior has been a bit of a concern lately."

"Lately? Mom, his drinking has been a concern for some time. He is just really good at hiding it. He was particularly well-behaved around you and Dad. He didn't want you to think poorly of him." She looked at her mom and realized she'd nodded in agreement. It surprised Kate that her mom would agree with her.

"There was a time that I thought Henry was a good match for you, but now I'm not so sure. I couldn't understand it, but after the accident he very seldom came to see you at the hospital. I thought he was so dedicated to you and loved you so much. That was before we were told about the amount of alcohol in his system. I think he felt guilty about the accident. It made me open my eyes." Maggie got up from the table and went back to the stove. "You know, about a year ago your dad said that there was something going on with Henry that bothered him. He wasn't sure what, but it put your dad off." She turned again and looked at her daughter. "Kate, are you sure you're ready to move out? It's no trouble having you stay with us. You know, Grammy loves to have you around."

"Mom, I do like being back in my old room, but I've got to get things settled and start living again. I go back to work at the end of the year and need to get into a routine again. And I can't live at home forever. I'm a big girl, you know?"

"I know. Don't remind me." She continued to stir the pot on the stove. "So are you going to have dinner with your friend again tonight?"

"No, not tonight. If there isn't enough food, I can scavenge through the cupboards," Kate said.

"There's enough. No scavenging." Her mom smiled at her. "We're having chili, cornbread and salad. I hope that will be acceptable."

"Acceptable? I was wondering what the good smell was. I need to remember to copy the recipe. Is Dad home yet?"

"Yeah, he's in the library and doing some work on a speech he'll present at the next board meeting."

Kate got up from the table. "I think I'll go bug him for a bit. I should tell him about the apartment." She left the kitchen and made her way down the hall. The door to the library was partly open. She peeked around the corner and saw her dad sat at his computer. He stared at the screen.

"Is that how speeches get written these days?" Kate asked.

Her dad seemed startled when he looked up. "Hi there, honey. Come on in and have a seat. I'm just editing. I should go on record now and say this will probably be one of the most boring speeches I've ever given. The markets have fluctuated lately and I can't nail down the final paragraph. Fortunately, I still have a couple of months to liven it up." He straightened in his chair and smiled at Kate. "So, we haven't talked for a few days. What's been going on?"

"Well, first the small news. I found an apartment. It's in the basement of a house out in Highwood. The people upstairs seem really nice. They're a retired couple. It's only ten miles from the university so the commute won't be too bad and should be convenient. It's time for me to get my own place and get ready to go back to work. I can't move in until the end of the week. I'm going to call U-Haul about a van. So, I'll be covered with newsprint and collecting boxes. I should be able to finish packing my things up by the end of the week."

Her dad leaned back in his chair. "Does Henry know?"

"I'm going to call him tonight and let him know."

"How do you think he'll take it?"

"It's hard to say. He seems to think we'll pick up where we left off before the accident, but I'm afraid it's been impossible to talk to him. I saw him at the townhouse and he wasn't particularly happy with me. So, I just have to make the move." Kate stood up and walked to a bookshelf. She peered at the books titles on the spines.

"He didn't hurt you?" Her dad stood up behind his desk and moved toward her.

"No." She glanced at him and didn't want to say that Henry pushed her against the car and bruised her arms. She also didn't want to tell her dad that she'd kneed him in the groin.

"What else is happening?"

She glanced at him again and then continued to look at the books.

"You're stalling," her dad said. "You said that was small news. Is there a bigger story?"

Kate turned around and looked at him. She leaned against the shelf and crossed her arms. "Now that you mention it, there is." She fell silent again and looked down at the carpet.

"You're still stalling," her dad said.

She moved back to the chair across from his desk and sat. "It's about Bill Leary," she finally said, and looked back at him. "It has to do with the dream." She waited to see if he would respond.

"The dream?" he replied.

"Yeah, funny thing there. Remember when I told you he'd been having the dreams about the same time period?"

107

"Yes, you said Bill has recurring dreams, too." Her dad moved to his desk, sat on the top, and looked at her.

"We've been discussing them - the dreams - and compared notes and memories. It's been really nice to have someone to talk to who understands them. It's weird though. We talk about the same dream, but from different perspectives - his and mine. Anyway, I told you about Connor and Lizzie dying in the fire and that I've always felt connected to the woman. Bill looks so much like Connor. We've been comparing memories of the dream and, Dad, it's really weird. In all the papers I've studied about dreams, not one says anything about two people having the same recurring dreams. When I first saw him I guess all the blood must have rushed to my head. I didn't pass out but got really dizzy. I'd gone through my life thinking the people in that dream didn't exist and then there he was. I was a little overwhelmed needless to say," Kate said.

"Needless to say." Her dad leaned forward and stood up. He walked around the room, and seemed to be lost in thought about what she'd said. He stopped and looked at her. "I figured that there was some kind of connection with your dreams and his, when you said he told you looked like the woman in his dream. Does Bill have any thoughts on what might be causing all this?"

"No, not really. We're both at a loss. And there's another really weird thing. Dad, you know some time ago when Grammy started to call me Lizzie, I asked her about it, but she wouldn't say anything about them. One morning last week, she called me Lizzie again and said more than she ever has about them. She talked about the day of the wedding, the fire, and how much I looked like her sister Elizabeth." Kate grimaced at her dad. "Weird, really weird, right? Your client, Dr. Stein, gave me the names of those parapsychologists who specialize in dreams and I left them a message a few days ago.

They finally called back today and Bill and I have an appointment for tomorrow."

"Do you think they might be able to help solve the puzzle?"

"We hope so. I know that for me it would be really nice to find out what it's supposed to mean. If there is any meaning, it seems like it should be significant that both of us have the same dream."

"Just be careful, okay? I know that if Neil gave you these people's names they should be reputable, but please be careful." He smiled down at her. "Hypnosis seems really scary. I'm certain I wouldn't be brave enough to try."

"We will be careful, I promise. I'm determined to take one step at a time."

"And keep me up to date. I want to hear what they have to report. It will be interesting to see if they know what could have caused you and Bill to be on the same plane."

"Dad, you're starting to sound like the Sci-Fi channel."

He chuckled. "You think I'm watching too much TV, like your mom." Just then her mom announce that dinner was ready. "Speaking of your mom, have you told her about all this?"

"I told her about the apartment, but not the other. I'm not sure how she'd respond. She always thought I was wasting time thinking about the dream. One small step at a time. I don't want to worry about upsetting her right now - at least, not until there is some reason for her to worry. I'm worried enough."

"Bill will be with you, right?" he asked.

"Yes."

"Then I don't think you should worry. Be excited about finding out the answers to all of this." He smiled as they moved toward the door.

"Always the scientist, Dad?" she asked.

"I may be an amateur, but you know I always had a dream of being more that a financial analyst." He gave her a kiss on the cheek.

Chapter Fourteen

That evening and the next day seemed to drag by for Kate. She felt excited about finally getting to the bottom of the dream, but she was also apprehensive. She thought the cliché about curiosity killing the cat related to her in a big way as to what these doctors might say about her and Bill's quandary. She was determined to go through with the consult. She tried to remember what she said to her dad about *one step at a time.*

She called Henry the night before and told him she would move her things out of the townhouse by the end of the week. She told him she'd try not to make too much of a mess - not that it would matter to him. There were times when they lived together that Kate didn't think housecleaning was in Henry's vocabulary.

She got up early and spent the morning at the townhouse. She rummaged through her things, cleaned out her closet and took things to the dumpster. It made her feel good. She threw out a lot of old stuff that no longer seemed important. She also collected several bags of clothes for donation that either didn't fit or she wasn't interested in wearing any longer. In her mind she felt that she'd made the right decision about the break up with Henry. She felt she'd turned a new corner and found she was very calm about the way life was headed.

Kate arranged to meet Bill at his house around one o'clock. The Sheridans' office was located in Everett, north of Seattle and, if traffic was bad on the freeway, it could take an hour or more just to get to Highwood. She finished for the time at the apartment, and left refreshed and ready for a new adventure. She got to Bill's exactly at one o'clock and they piled into his truck and headed for the freeway. It started to rain that morning, so the traffic was heavy and slow. It made for a great time for small talk during the car ride, but they were silent for most of it. They arrived in Everett at 1:45 and found the doctors' offices. They entered a small waiting room that was painted and furnished in calm colors. Light browns and pale yellows were the hue of the day in the room. There was a big overstuffed sofa and a couple of armchairs arranged nicely in the outer office. They sat side by side on the sofa. Kate knew the furniture was there to make people feel comfortable, but she felt less calm than before. She began to doubt her decision to go there. She and Bill filled out some forms and then they waited.

Bill reached over and placed his hand on her arm. "Are you nervous?" he asked.

"How could you tell?" Kate answered.

"You have that look on your face." He smiled at her.

"Which look would that be?"

"You know, the one you got before the wedding," he replied and then his brows furled and he looked at her strangely. "Wait a minute. What did I just say?"

Kate leaned back on the sofa and thought, *now I really feel nervous.*

They sat in silence and stared at one another until a woman in a white coat entered the room. "Hi, I'm Robin, the doctor's assistant. I spoke with you on the phone to make the appointment," she said and smiled. "Follow me."

Kate and Bill followed her into another part the building. They entered an average sized office with two desks. The nameplate on the door read, Anna Sheridan, M.D. and Jeff Sheridan Ph.D.

Robin motioned them to two chairs and asked if she could get them coffee or tea. Kate asked for coffee and so did

Bill, and then she looked around the room. There were a couple of paintings on the walls, along with plaques with degrees and certificates. Robin returned with their coffees and said the doctors would be with them in a minute.

Bill again reached over and placed his hand on Kate's arm. "I don't know where that came from, or I do know where that came from." He shook his head. "I know it was strange. I didn't mean to frighten you."

Kate focused on her cup of coffee. "You didn't really frighten me. It just caught me a little off guard." She tried to smile at him, but couldn't. She started to say something else, but two people entered the room behind them. They introduced themselves as Anna and Jeff. He laughed and said they didn't thrive on formalities and would it be okay if they all went by first names. Kate could tell he tried to make them feel comfortable, but after what Bill said about the look on her face, she felt uneasy. Anna and Jeff pulled the chairs out from behind their desks and seated themselves.

Anna started things off. "When I received your email I found your story very interesting. Being there are two of you having the same progressive dreams is very exciting. We will want to separate after a bit, but why don't we just start at the beginning?" She looked expectantly at them.

Kate knew the woman wanted information, but she felt uneasy. "Why separate?" she asked. "I don't think I like that idea." She looked at Bill.

"It might help determine where the story is coming from," Jeff answered.

"Story? Might help?" Kate looked back at them. "This isn't a story from some book or movie. This is something that really happened." She felt her unease build and thought she should run from the room. She saw Bill look at her and felt a little startled by the look on his face. He reached over and took her hand.

"Let me explain," Anna said. "We do dream therapy, but it is usually with only one patient. We've never had sessions that included two people having the same dream. This is a bit new for us. We don't want you to feel uneasy. If separating doesn't work, we can do this together. We do want to help," Anna said, and looked directly at Kate.

Bill nodded and said, "We understand." He looked at Kate and nodded his head again. She squeezed his hand and watched him look back to the doctors. He cleared his throat. "I'm not really sure where to begin. I started having a dream when I was a kid. It was like a serial. Every dream ended and then continued about some other kid. It followed him as he grew up in Ireland and, later, when he came to America. The dream was about everything he did." Bill looked at Kate.

"I started to have the dream when I was a kid, too, only from a different angle," Kate said.

"Different, how?" Jeff asked.

"It was from a different person's life, I guess. The dreams continued up until recently. I was in a motor vehicle accident over Labor Day and I had the last dream while I was in the hospital. That was the first week of September," Kate answered.

"My dreams also stopped in September. In fact it was the same day...I mean both of us had the dream end on the same day," Bill added.

"This isn't making any sense," Kate said and felt confused.

"Let's back up just a little," Jeff said calmly. "How old were you when the dreams started?"

She looked at Bill and then back at Jeff. "I don't remember an exact age, but the first time I can say that it stuck with me I was maybe four or five," Kate answered.

"Is that the same for you Bill?" he asked.

"Yeah, about that time," Bill responded. "The dream is in another time and place. I'd see through a child's eyes, and grow up with him. He grew up in Ireland and then came over to America on a ship with his wife. I think he was about seventeen-years-old. His wife died on the ship, and he traveled around the eastern part of the US, then decided to come west. He settled in the Seattle area where he met Elizabeth. They fell in love, married and died. Then one day I was working on a car and it turned out the owner was Kate who was Elizabeth in the dream. It's all rather confusing."

"Was it pretty much the same for you, Kate?" Anna asked.

"Yes, only I watched Elizabeth grow up. The other strange part of this is that we've found out that Elizabeth and Connor were distant relatives of ours. Elizabeth was my great-aunt. My grandmother had a sister who died in a fire on her wedding night. It was in 1912. My grandmother calls me Lizzie once in a while and the other day she really spoke about it in detail. Before that, she'd always been reluctant to discuss Lizzie."

"My grandfather was from Ireland. He came to America in the 1920's and had a brother who came over before him. The brother disappeared and was never heard from again. I did some family research and found that Connor was my grandfather's brother. He used to talk about this brother who was lost to the family. They never knew what happened to him," Bill said.

"Connor is the man in my dreams, but Bill looks just like him." Kate looked at Bill. "I feel like I'm getting ahead of myself here."

Anna smiled at them and said, "Let's take this one step at a time." Kate latched on to that cliché and started to feel calmer. "You said the dream started to occur when you were children and continued until recently?" Anna asked. Both Kate and Bill nodded. Anna looked at Jeff and he nodded. "It sounds more like a progressive dream, rather than a recurring."

"You called it progressive when we first came in. What's the difference?" Kate asked.

"Recurring dreams are the same scenario happening over and over. A progressive dream continues a story - chapters one, two, three and such." Anna smiled. "What kind of changes have occurred?"

Kate and Bill looked at each other. "Ladies first," Bill said.

"Well," Kate started and took in a deep breath. "When I was a kid, I mostly dreamt about West Seattle. I'd walk down the main street or by the bay. I'd look at the sky and watch the birds and ducks. I remember I'd see things in the house where I lived. There was a piano in the main living room and French doors that went out into a hallway. I never really saw anything other than that until I turned twelve or thirteen. Then I started to see people and they began to talk to me. They would call me Elizabeth or Lizzie and I'd wake up knowing that was wrong, but there have been times when I wasn't sure. Was it me or Elizabeth? Was I Elizabeth? I wasn't sure what to think."

"I've felt the same way," Bill added. "When Connor's wife died on the crossing from Ireland I was sad for weeks. I've never been sure about the meaning of things that appear in the dream and who I represent."

"Have you ever thought of reincarnation?" Jeff asked.

"We've discussed it a little, but since we don't have a very good understanding of that phenomenon we thought it better to wait before we make up our minds," Bill said.

"There has been a lot of scientific study done on the subject, and not just the stuff you see in the rag papers at the grocery checkout. You know, the Dali Llama from Tibet is supposed to be reincarnated from the previous Dali. There have been reports of children on the other side of the world identifying people in the United States as past relations. They're able to relate family stories and names of people in the past. We've had some proof with past life hypnosis of people currently living who were here before."

Kate felt skeptical. "Yeah, but what about the reports of people getting information fed into their heads during hypnosis? That they were abused by their parents or abducted by aliens? Bill said a while back that anything is possible, but I'm not sure I believe in it."

"Those reports are true," Anna said. "There are some practitioners out there who aren't very reputable - your basic scam artists - and they lead their clients down false paths. We can assure you that we are in this specifically for the knowledge. We won't plant any ideas in your head."

"I don't mean to offend, but if we were to do hypnosis I'd really prefer to have Bill stay in the room at the same time," Kate said.

"That won't be a problem...and no offense taken." Jeff smiled at her. "We understand that you might have misgivings about this form of therapy. Anna and I will compare notes, but I think I can say that regression hypnosis could answer a lot of the questions and ease your mind. The sub-conscious sometimes keeps us from remembering things that could be dangerous to remember. It likes to protect us from ourselves. With hypnosis we can open up the subconscious and find out things we never knew occurred."

Kate and Bill looked at each other and she nodded at him. "We've discussed doing hypnosis and we both think it's a little on the scary side. We would like to try, though."

"We usually schedule sessions to start around one in the afternoon and allow two to four hours. If we're going to hypnotize both of you in one day we'll have to allow at least four hours. Let me get Robin. She can help us find a day that will work," Anna said and got up from her seat.

"There are some things you should talk about before our next appointment. There are pros and cons to hypnosis like everything else in the world. We'll have you sign consent forms and you'll need to decide if you want to remember everything after the session." Jeff got up and went to one of the desks. He opened a drawer and pulled out a couple of booklets. "Here is some reading material for you. Read it and discuss it so that you'll feel comfortable with the decision you make. If you have any apprehension we need to get those sorted out before we hypnotize you. If you have any questions before your session we allow time to answer those, so write them down. We want you both to be as comfortable and sure as possible, okay?"

***

Bill and Kate scheduled their first hypnosis session for the next Thursday, just a week away. They walked out of the office and down to the truck silently. They got in and sat for a few minutes. Bill put the key in the ignition, but when he started to turn it Kate put her hand on his and stopped him.

"How did you find finally telling someone else?" he asked.

"Good in a way, but I'm scared." Kate surprised herself by starting to cry. She looked at him. She saw he had a worried look on his face. He reached his hand up to her face and touched one of the tears that rolled down her cheek. "I know it's going to be good to get this out. It's good to be building some sort of understanding, but I feel so out there. I didn't think it would be so unsettling," she said between sobs. "Bill, I'm usually pretty level-headed. This seems so unreal. If my mom knew about this she'd have a fit."

"Is your mom a realist?"

"Yeah, big time."

Bill took her hand and put it to his lips. "I understand what you're saying." He rested his cheek on her hand. "What seems even stranger is I don't feel I know who I am anymore. I

118

look at you and I'm not sure who I'm looking at. I feel like I've known you all my life. Which life? It must be Connor's; we only met a week ago, right? I don't think I ever really knew how much I wasn't aware of until lately." He wiped the tears from her face and looked her in the eyes. "I was really relieved when you said you wanted me to stay in the room when they hypnotize you. I feel the same. I do know we're both very strong and we can get through this. We're going to find answers and maybe some truths. We can do that, don't you think?"

Kate swallowed hard. She pulled a tissue out of her purse and blew her nose. She closed her eyes and tried to relax. "Bill, how do you feel about hypnosis now?" She opened her eyes and watched him.

He grimaced and crossed his eyes. "I know it will open another door, but it scares me, too. I wonder what will be on the other side."

"Maybe something from a Wes Craven film?" Kate asked. He nodded yes. "There goes the realist in me. I feel like we're planning to have brain surgery."

"I'm not so into the brain surgery idea." He smiled and started to laugh. It was the kind of laugh that spreads and Kate caught it. Every time they looked at each other they'd laugh that much harder.

"Now I do feel hysterical," she said, as she calmed down.

"I'd say we needed that," Bill said and smiled at her.

Kate reached up and touched his lips. "I think I can see what Elizabeth saw in you. She loved your smile." Kate suddenly realized what she'd said and pulled her hand back. "Sorry, now I'm doing it."

"Doing what?"

"Being weird. Are you hungry?" she asked and cleared her throat. She tried to be serious.

He turned the key in the truck's ignition and put it in reverse. "When I'm really nervous, I eat. Would you like some ice cream?"

Chapter Fifteen

The next Thursday came up fast for Kate. She put off her move for a week since there were no rental vans available anywhere in the city.

In the days prior, they read the pamphlets, got online and discussed hypnosis late into the night. During the day when Bill taught his class and met with students, Kate continued to get things ready for the move. She felt continual nagging about the hypnosis session and Bill said he wasn't giving it his all in class and during his student meetings; he'd cut them off early and send them on their way. She found if she stared out the window it would help some, but her mind always came back to Lizzie and Connor. Bill mentioned he wasn't paying attention to what the other teachers said in staff meetings and in the garage pits, where he knew every inch of any given situation with a car, he found it difficult to focus on the problems. When Bill said he felt out of control, Kate agreed. It was difficult to keep track of what she was supposed to think about.

The owners of the house where Kate planned to move gave her the keys to the basement apartment early. She packed up a few loads into her car and dropped them off. She did as much as she could physically. After a couple of trips up and down the stairs at the apartment, she'd tire out and her hip got stiff. She'd quit early in the afternoon and take a nap before she'd leave to meet Bill. She hadn't seen anything of Henry. She felt they should talk again, but was glad, in a way, that he hadn't been around.

On Tuesday afternoon, she'd loaded several of the boxes and suitcases into her car with the intention of taking them to the new apartment, but she felt tired and decided to head over to Bill's. She found him grading papers and when she saw her at the door, he enveloped her in a warm bear hug.

"Your car seems to be filled with boxes," he said.

She turned in his arms and looked at her VW. "Yeah, I was going to drop them off at the new place, but ran out of steam."

He turned her back to him and continued the hug. "How about we have a nice quiet dinner out somewhere?"

She smiled and looked up at him. "That's a nice idea. Would it be okay if I took a nap for about an hour first? I need to recharge my batteries."

"No problem. I have a nice big comfy couch you can crash on while I finish grading." He led her into the living room and got her settled on the couch.

Kate scrunched down and thought about how lucky she was to have found Bill. He was caring and thoughtful and sweet and about nine hundred other adjectives she could think of to describe him. She lay on the couch and smiled and then thought about everything she needed to do before Saturday. She'd have to make one more trip back to the townhouse and get the donation bags out of there. Her brain began to spin, but she dozed off.

They had a nice dinner that evening and Bill convinced her that everything would be ready to go by the move on Saturday. After dinner, he helped her unload the boxes into the new apartment and made her promise not to over-do the packing again.

She went back to the townhouse a couple more times that week and tried not to leave a big mess. She debated constantly about things she packed. Most of the kitchen paraphernalia was hers, but she didn't want to leave Henry empty-handed. When she finally gave up on the second day, she felt fairly sure she had just about everything packed. She'd pick up the truck on Saturday, get the few pieces of furniture packed with help from her dad, Bill and a couple of friends from work, and say goodbye to that part of her life.

On Thursday, as before, Kate got to Bill's at noon and they headed north to Everett. They didn't say much on the way. Kate kept her eyes on the road and talked to herself as Bill drove. She wanted to stay calm, but she felt on edge. She also felt a little skeptical that Anna and Jeff would be able to get her under hypnosis.

They arrived at the offices and got out of the truck. They looked at each other and Kate shrugged her shoulders. "We have nothing to lose? Right?" She tried to smile.

"Right, right," Bill answered. He took her hand and they walked into the office building.

They were shown into Anna and Jeff's office by their assistant Robin again and both sat down. Then Bill got back up and scooted his chair closer to Kate's. He sat back down and put his hand on hers. She curled her fingers through his and smiled.

Anna and Jeff entered the room. They spent fifteen minutes explaining the session in-depth to Kate and Bill. They went over the pros and cons. Anna asked if they wanted to remember everything and they both answered yes. They'd discussed it the night before and decided what was the use of being hypnotized if they wouldn't remember it? They signed consent forms. Jeff asked if they felt comfortable enough to be in separate rooms. Bill and Kate looked at each other and both said *no* emphatically. They explained to the doctors that they had discussed it and they both wanted to hear everything. Anna got up, softened the lights in the room and put on some quiet music. Jeff asked who would go first.

Bill stood up and said, "That would be me. Do I lie down or what?"

Jeff smiled and said, "I guess you two did discuss this. That's your choice. You can relax on the recliner over there," he pointed to the corner. "Or you can stay in the chair here."

"There's not any chance I'll fall out of the chair or anything?" Bill asked. Kate understood why he felt a little thrown off by the over-stuffed chair. It was imposing. "Did you just move the recliner in here? I don't remember it from the other day."

"There's always a chance you could slide out of the regular chair. The recliner has sat there for a couple of years. Maybe it would be more comfortable." Jeff got up and moved to a chair by the recliner.

Anna walked over to Kate and looked down at her. "Let's move these chairs over to the other side of the room. No offense meant, but there shouldn't be any distractions. You'll be able to hear everything." Kate nodded and got up to move the chair.

And so it begins, Kate thought. *We're heading down a road that's waited for us for a long time.* She realized it involved not only their lives, but the lives of their families.

Chapter Sixteen

Bill took his coat off and sat in the recliner. He pushed back and stretched out his legs. His feet dangled over the edge of the foot rest, he was so tall. After he moved around a little to get himself comfortable, Bill took in a deep breath and tried to relax.

Jeff sat in the chair facing Bill. "Okay, before we start I'd like for you to stand up and have a good stretch. I know you just sat down, but this will help you get your blood pressure down."

Bill stood and stretched his arms up and could just about touch the ceiling. He looked over at Kate, who sat across the room with Anna, and winked at her.

"That's great. Work out all the kinks; take in a couple of deep breaths. Good, stretch your neck. Good. Okay, sit back down and make yourself comfortable. Close your eyes and take in another couple of deep breaths. Nice. Now fill your lungs and exhale completely. I've got a quarter here in my hand and I'm going to put it onto your palm."

Bill felt the cool metal in his hand.

"Don't close your hand around it. Just focus on the feel of it. Good. Take in a breath and feel yourself relax. Now, this time, take in a deep breath and hold it. Focus on the quarter and with your eyes closed, feel yourself relax and begin to drift. Feel like you are floating on the air. Now let your breath out and feel the air move around you. It's just a light warm breeze. In a few minutes I'll ask you to open your eyes, but your lids will be so heavy you won't be able to open them."

Bill almost started to laugh, but found he couldn't. He could feel the warm breeze move around his body. He felt at peace.

"Bill, please, try to open your eyes." He heard Jeff say from very far away.

"I can't open them."

"Good. Now please lift your right arm."

"I can't."

"Good. We're going to travel back in time. Let's go back ten years ago. Can you see yourself?"

He realized he could see where he was very clearly. "Yes."

"Where are you?"

"I'm in college in Seattle," Bill said. He felt as he did when he was younger.

"What are you studying?"

"Mostly automotive repair and teaching, but I'm finishing a rotation in general garage maintenance and to get my degree I have to take math and English."

"Okay, we'll continue back another couple of years. Can you see yourself?"

"Yes."

"Where are you?"

"Everett, Washington."

"Is that where you were born?"

"Yes."

"How old are you?"

"Sixteen." He felt amazed by all he could see around him. It was just as he remembered from his teens - the house, the yard, everything looked so bright and real.

"What are you doing?" He heard Jeff ask the questions from far away.

"I just got my driver's license and my stepdad let me drive the car home. I parked it crooked in the driveway, but he said it was okay."

"Bill, we're going to continue back. As the time slips by, tell me what you see. I want you to know that nothing here will hurt you. It may appear strange, but you'll just watch it. What do you see?"

"Birthdays and Christmas. My mom and stepdad are getting younger. I'm playing baseball, spending the night with school friends. Picnics. Vacations. I can't move and everything seems really clear. My mom smiles at me. She looks so young. My dad - my real dad - holds me and walks around the house."

"Bill, continue back. What do you see?"

"Nothing. It's gotten dark. No wait, there's a light. I can hear a voice." He could hear someone else speak. It wasn't Jeff and he began to feel scared.

"What is the voice saying?"

Bill tried very hard to understand what he heard the voice say. "I can't really hear it; I just know it's there. The light is getting brighter. The voice is saying something about it not being the time and I'll have to forgive."

"Does what the voice says make any sense to you?"

"No, just that it isn't the right time and I smell smoke. There's Lizzie. God, she's so beautiful."

"Bill, remember nothing will hurt you. Clear your mind and move back to an even earlier time. Find the time before you traveled to Seattle, before you met Elizabeth, before the fire. Where are you?"

"I'm in New York." Bill felt different. He could hear the voice come out of him, but it wasn't his. The Irish accent was thick and he felt more alert and on guard.

"What are you doing?"

"I'm trying to live my life. I miss my wife. It's only been a year since I lost her on the ship."

"What is the name of your wife?"

"Fiona."

"How did you lose her?"

"She got sick on the crossing from Ireland. The doctor on the ship called it the croup. A lot of the people on board the ship got it and died. It was so cold on the boat, no one could get warm."

"What kind of work do you do in New York?"

"I do just about anything. I got a job at a steel mill. Never did it before, but they were willing to train me."

"What is your name?"

"Connor O'Leary."

"Why are you smiling?"

"There's this old guy, named Sid, nice man. He's teaching me, after we get off work, how to put shoes on horses. He's teaching me a lot about iron. Once, when we have the day off from the mill, he invites me out to his house for supper. His wife is a pretty good cook. Sid shows me the things he's made out of iron. He says he can teach me to do this kind of work, too."

"Why does that make you smile?"

"He reminds me a bit of my da. Sid's a good man."

"Okay, you're going to move slowly forward. Let's go to the time you decided to leave New York. Why did you decide to leave?"

"It's too big of a city and dirty. It's noisy all the time. There are different gangs on the streets and if you don't watch out, they'll steal the shoes off your feet. I was approached by the Irish and they wanted me to join them in defendin' their part of the city. I wasn't havin' any of it. Where I come from isn't like this and I don't like it. I'm not comfortable here. The people aren't very kind and I get called names."

"Connor, where are you from originally?"

"Cork, Ireland."

"What year is it?"

"1909." Bill heard the words that came out of his mouth and, although, he could remember everything he said, it all seemed so very strange.

"How did you decide to head west to Seattle?"

"There's a pub down the street from the boarding house where I live. It's a nickel a pint and they have pretty fair food. Usually on Friday, after we get paid, the lads from the mill and me, we go there to toss a couple down. One day this guy named Fred Smalley starts to talk about how he is going to head west to a place called Oregon. He's leaving in a couple of months with his family and he wants to know if there is anybody interested in going along. I talk to him for a bit and find out he's looking for somebody to share the costs. He needs somebody to just help out. He says there is more land in Oregon than you could possibly fill up in a lifetime and the land is cheap and there are plenty of places to work until the funds are raised to buy your own acreage. I tell him I'm more than interested, that he can count me in. Over the year and a half I've been in New York, I've saved up as much money as I can. I'll be able to help some with the costs. We shake on it and he tells me we're to leave in April, three months' time."

"Let's move forward again to the day you leave. How are you traveling?"

"We're taking the train to Chicago. Then we'll buy horses and a wagon to take the rest of the way out. The train ride is going to be tough."

"Why is it going to be tough?"

"It's a two-day trip. Sitting up all that way will make me stiff in the back."

"Move forward again to arriving in Seattle. What do you see?"

"Oh, it's such a lovely town here. There are mountains and the water and the skies as blue as precious stones when

you can see it. It rains a lot, but it reminds me of Cork. Seattle is bigger than I thought it'd be, but quiet and the people smile at you."

"Why didn't you stay in Oregon?"

"I had a hard time finding work. I was at a saloon in Portland and heard there were jobs up north in Seattle, mostly working timber. I thought I'd give it a chance."

"What kind of work did you find?"

"When I got into town I did odd jobs for a while. I heard about a livery stable in West Seattle looking for help. I walked down there and met the boss, Jack Hutch. He tested me, watched me shoe a couple of ponies, and then gave me the job."

"How long did you work for him?"

"After I'd been there a few months, I asked him if I could partner up with him. I tried to save money all the time, so had a little extra. I still had some of the money left over from the trip west and was going to use it for buying land. Jack thought about it and agreed. So we partnered up. That winter was terrible. Jack was riding into work one cold, icy morning and his horse slipped. He hit his head and died. His wife said for me to take over the stable, she wanted nothing to do with it. So it was mine."

"What year is it?"

"1911."

"Find the time and tell me about when you first saw Elizabeth."

"She's a lovely lass. I'd see her every now and again when she'd walk down the street toward the schoolhouse. I found out she's the teacher. She always walked with two other girls. I'd watched her go by the stables; never thought she noticed me a bit. One day I was in front of the stable, can't even remember what I was doing, and she came toward me all by herself. I was frozen stiff, because she looked right at me. She smiled and waved. I somehow got my hand up to wave back. She crossed the street and came over to where I stood. She said, *hi, I'm Elizabeth MacDiarmid.* I stuttered and finally got my name out. She said something about there being a picnic lunch on Sunday, put on by the church and she hoped I'd be able to attend. I hardly heard her. It was all I could do to keep my mouth from hanging down. She is so beautiful. She isthe school teacher and the two other girls usually with her were her sisters."

"Did you make it to the picnic?"

"You bet and did I have a grand time. The people in this town are so nice and friendly."

"Tell me what did you do and what do you see around you at the picnic?"

Bill felt himself laugh. "Over yonder, there's a round of horseshoes being played by some of the old timers. There's a big barbeque pit where a pig is being roasted, chickens, too. The ladies have tables set up with foods of every type on them. I'm introduced to a lot of new people and am havin' a terrible time remembering names."

"Did you get to talk to Elizabeth?"

"Yes."

"What do you talk about?"

"Oh, just light things. The weather and what we do for work. She really likes teaching school. She introduces me to her family."

"Do you remember the family member's names?"

"Yes. Her mother's name is Mae, and her father is Daniel. He has a strong handshake. Seems like a good man. Her older sister is Delia, she's married to a man named Thomas. The two younger sisters are Effie and Winnona."

"Let's move forward again. Do you remember the day you asked Elizabeth to marry you?"

"Aye, that I do."

"Where are you?"

"We're sitting on the front porch of her parents' house. I tell her that I want to ask her father for permission. She says yes. I'm so happy. It's the first really happy day I've had in a long time. I'm also the luckiest man in West Seattle."

"Tell me about your wedding night."

"Someone is shaking me awake. Elizabeth is shaking me and saying fire. Now I can smell the smoke. I've got to get her to safety. We've got to get out of here. The smoke is so thick." Bill felt his throat tighten and coughed. "We head out to the hallway, but the smoke is too dense out there, so we go back to the room. We go to the window and I see that the overhang beneath our window is on fire. I tell Elizabeth we've got to try the hallway and we move out of the room. At the top of the stairs I see a path down the middle that isn't on fire. We start to go down. Something happens and I'm falling."

"What is happening? Connor, what is happening?

"It's dark. There's a light up ahead and I can hear someone say it's not the right time."

"Okay, I'm going to count from one to ten. You'll start to come back to the present time. You will feel safe, comfortable and rested. You will remember all that we have talked about in the session. One, two, three, four, five...you're coming closer to the present time. You feel calm and can breathe freely. The quarter is getting lighter in your hand. Six, seven, eight, nine, ten...you are now in the present. You will remember everything you've just witnessed. I will snap my fingers and you will open your eyes. How do you feel Bill?"

Bill opened his eyes and sat up quickly. He looked at Jeff. "What?"

"How do you feel?"

"Odd."

"Why odd?"

Bill shook his head. "I don't know. I'm not sure what to make of that voice talking about it not being the right time. I could see that bright light, but I don't think I could go there." He pushed the foot rest down and planted his feet on the ground. "I don't think I'm making very much sense."

"I'm not sure about that voice either. I'm interested to see if Kate has a similar experience. Let's see what we find out from her. We'll allow time for a discussion after Kate's session."

Bill noticed that Kate held a tissue to her nose and it was obvious she'd been crying. He moved to her and squatted down in front of her. "Hey, are you okay?" He took her hand.

"Yeah, I'm just remembering when I woke up in the hospital. It was the last dream and it was really upsetting, knowing they or we died. Hearing you talk about it just brought the memories back." She smiled and squeezed his hand. "I'm all right."

Chapter Seventeen

Jeff sat down in the chair next to the recliner and put his hand on Kate's arm. "Do you have any questions?"

"I'm a little...well, I'm nervous, but I'm good to go."

Like Bill, she stood and stretched as she did when she got out of bed in the morning. She'd taken in the deep breaths, until she felt dizzy. Jeff put the quarter in her hand.

"Are you comfortable Kate?" he asked. She nodded. "Okay, take in some more deep breaths and let them out slowly. Good. Close your eyes and continue to breathe. Do it again and relax. Try to listen to the air as it enters and departs your lungs. Feel yourself float. It's peaceful. Focus on the weight of the quarter in the palm of your hand. In a moment, I'll ask you to stand up, but you won't be able to. Your body will feel very heavy and relaxed. Kate, please stand up."

She tried to push herself up from the recliner, but felt heavy. "I can't."

"Can you lift you left arm and hold it up?"

"It won't move."

"Good. Kate, we're going to go back one year in your life. Can you tell me where you are?"

She looked around, and saw her office at the university. "I'm at work."

"Where do you work?"

"The University of Washington Hospital in Social Services."

"Are you a social worker?"

"Yes."

"Do you like that work?"

134

"Yes, very much. I like to help the patients and their families, particularly the elderly."

"Okay, now we're going to go back six years. The years are going back. Can you tell me where you are?"

"I'm at Gonzaga University." Kate saw the campus. She walked to class.

"What are you studying?"

"I want to be a teacher, but I've recently started thinking about changing my major. I've been researching social work and I think I may go in that direction."

"Where do you live?"

"In the student housing apartments."

"Good. Now we're going to travel back another ten years. Can you tell me where you are?"

"I'm at home, doing my homework."

"How old are you?"

"Nine."

"What homework are you studying?"

"Math. Ick. Yuck. I'm not doing so well in math. I like English and we have a really nice teacher. My mom makes me study in the kitchen while she cooks dinner. She thinks I'm not studying hard enough in my room."

"Let's continue back another ten years. The time will be going by. You'll see birthdays and Christmas mornings. You'll see yourself as a baby lying in the crib. Do you see these things?"

"Yes."

"Continue back. Kate, I want you to know nothing here will hurt you. You have nothing to be afraid of as you go back in time. What do you see?"

"Darkness. There's a beam of light, like a star floating over there. I can hear somebody mumbling."

"Can you hear what they're saying?"

"No. I don't think I'm supposed to be here. The light moves away from me and I can smell smoke. I can see Connor. It's very hot." Kate felt panic set in deep in her stomach. She found it hard to breathe and started to suck in air.

"Nothing is going to hurt you, Kate. Let's continue back a few years to the day you first noticed Connor. What is going on around you?"

Kate begins to feel calm again and realizes she walks a street in West Seattle. "I'm on my way to school. I'm a teacher. My sisters Effie and Winnona are with me. They're both in my class at the school. It bothers them to have to call me Miss MacDiarmid. Effie is particularly disturbed by it. She's not quite two years younger than me and it really bothers her. Every day we walk past Mr. Hutch's livery stable and I notice a new man works for him. He is certainly handsome. He has dark hair, and blue eyes. He smiles at us as we walk by."

"What is your name?"

"Elizabeth MacDiarmid."

"Do you remember the first time you spoke to Connor?"

"Yes. The reverend at church announced there would be a spring picnic in a couple of weeks. I decided to ask the man if he would like to attend. One morning, when we walked to school, I asked Effie and Winnona to go on ahead. I said I'd only be a few minutes. I crossed the road in front of the livery and found him at work. I think I startled him, but introduced myself. He told me his name is Connor O'Leary and then I invited him to the picnic."

"What did he say?"

"He said yes, it would be nice to meet some of the people in West Seattle. He has such a nice smile and a very intriguing accent. I asked him where he is from originally and he said Ireland. I had to get to school, but think I'll ask him how he came to be in Seattle, when he comes for the picnic."

"Let's move forward now to a year after your first meeting. What is happening?"

"I can smell outdoor fragrances. There's a fish odor coming from the bay. The tide is out and the sun has made it a very warm day. The smell is coming from there. It is such a beautiful day, everything looks so green. I can see the azaleas in bloom."

"Where are you?"

"We are at Alki Point. I'm walking with Connor. He picks some wild flowers for me."

"Are you there for any particular reason?"

"We walked to the Point after church for a picnic. It's just the two of us. There's a blanket under a cedar tree. I made fried chicken and cornbread. He seems to like the cornbread very much."

"Tell me about the picnic. What is happening?"

"Connor holds my hand and runs his finger over the ring he gave me. I think he spent every penny he earned on it. He seems very serious and says he's so happy he asked my father for permission to marry me. He asks if it will be very hard to put up with him. I feel such joy fill my heart that I almost start to cry. I tell him when I said yes, it was an acceptance of him as is and give him a hug. He asks if it's okay to give me a kiss. I tell him yes, again, and he gives me the sweetest kiss. My heart races in my chest. It isn't the first time he's kissed me, but this is a special moment. When I open my eyes, I notice someone stands behind a tree nearby. I know who's there and watches us."

"Who is it?"

"It's my younger sister, Effie. I shout at her, 'Effie are you spying on us?' I apologize to Connor and stand up. As I walk toward her, I can see that she is crying. I ask her why she is crying. Has she hurt herself?"

"Does she give you an answer?"

"Yes, she starts shouting, 'I hate you, I hate you.' She says I stole Connor from her. She curses me and says she hopes God will think badly of me. She hopes God will curse me and my children forever. Then she runs away down the beach. I turn back to Connor. He'd folded up the blanket and gathered up the rest of our picnic items."

"How do you feel about what Effie said?"

"I knew she had a crush on Connor, but I didn't think it would make her hate me. I decide then and there that I'll talk to her that evening. We need to get it straightened out. I don't want there to be any bad feelings. I'm engaged to Connor. He shouldn't feel uncomfortable being with any of my family. I also don't want him to feel he has caused a rift between my sister and me."

"Did you speak with her that evening?"

"No. After Connor left to go back to the stables, I spoke with my mother about what happened. My mother said she will talk to Effie and see if she can get it sorted out."

"Let's move forward to your wedding day. How do you feel? Are you nervous?"

"Yes, I'm very happy, but also nervous. The day seems to fly by so quickly. Everyone is cheerful. The weather turned out beautiful. Someone spiked the punch with alcohol, but the ladies from the church see to it right away and it is replaced. I think I was silly for worrying so. My mother and the other ladies have moved mountains to see that everything goes well."

"Tell me what happens after the wedding and reception? Where did you go for your honeymoon?"

"My father reserved a suite for us at the Broadview Hotel. It's situated near the beach and is so wonderful. Fresh flowers are in the vases. The room is very lovely and warm."

"And your relations with Connor. How did that go?"

"He is the gentlest man I've ever met. He knows I'm nervous, but isn't pushy at all. He's very kind and we find many things to laugh about."

"After the relations what happens?"

Kate felt the panic set in, again. "I smell smoke and wake Connor up. I put on a dressing gown and some slippers. He's looking out the window and says there is smoke coming out of the front of the building. He grabs my hand and leads me to the door. When we walk into the hallway the smoke is very thick. We go back into the room. It's very difficult to breathe. We go back to the window and see the wooden overhang beneath the window blazing. I see people run with buckets in the street. I go to the other window and the smoke rises. I can see the shadow of someone standing in between the hotel and the building next to it. Connor says we'll have to try the stairs and so we go back into the hallway. From the top of the stairwell, we can see an opening down the middle of the stairs and we head down. We are about half way, when one of the stairs gives way under my feet. I'm falling and hit the wooden floor below. I can hear boards splitting. I land on top of Connor. When I push up I can see his beautiful eyes staring straight up. He isn't breathing and I know he's dead. I look around and see flames snap and dance all around me. I put my hand over his eyes to close the lids and then put my head back down on his chest and wait. The thought of not having him in my life is impossible. I don't want to even try to think about it." Kate cried and coughed at the same time, it became so difficult to breath.

"Okay, we're going to move forward to the present time. I'll count one to ten and you'll come back. You'll feel safe and comfortable and remember everything you witnessed. One, two, three, four, five...you're coming closer to the present time. You feel calm and can breathe freely. Six, seven, eight, nine, ten...you are now in the present. I will snap my fingers and you will open your eyes. How do you feel Kate?"

"I...Bill..." She looked across the room and Bill was no longer in the chair. She looked around the room and saw him by a window with his back to her.

She felt strangely close to him, but also far away. Jeff sat down in the chair next to Kate and smiled at her and she sees Anna at her desk scribbling notes. "Bill?"

He finally turned from the window. She saw a tear run down his cheek. He cleared his throat. "Jeff, could you guys give us a minute here?"

Jeff nodded and stood. He held his hand out to Anna and they left the office.

Kate could see the serious look in his eyes. "Bill, what is the matter?" she asked.

"Why didn't you get out of there? You were still alive; you had a chance to live."

Kate pushed forward in the recliner and looked down at her hands. "I think I said why. I couldn't live without you. I loved you more than anything."

"But, Elizabeth, you could have lived," Bill said. He moved around a chair and squatted down in front of her. He placed his hands on her thighs. He put his hand up to her cheek. "You could have survived."

"I know. I didn't want to. I couldn't face life without you," she said and placed her hands over his.

"Tell me you didn't suffer. Tell me..." He choked and put his head on her knees. "Tell me you didn't feel any pain."

"No, no I didn't. I think I must have passed out from the smoke or the heat. I don't know," she said, quietly. She brought her hand up and ran it through his dark hair. "Bill, was that us? I remember it so vividly. It was as clear as anything."

He looked back up at her and wiped his cheek. "I can still smell the smoke. I'll go get Jeff and Anna." He stood and started to turn, but stopped.

Kate looked up as he bent at the waist and put his hand around the back of her neck. He leaned over to kiss her and she wrapped her arms around his shoulders. He pulled her up and off her feet. Their lips melded together and tongues swirled as passion overtook her for a fleeting moment.

Bill slowed the kiss, which became gentle and soft. He let her down onto her feet and she looked up into his beautiful blue eyes. "Go get them. I have some questions," she said. "And then I want out of here."

Chapter Eighteen

Jeff sat at his desk. Bill felt him watch as he and Kate moved the chairs back. Anna leaned against his desk.

"I think there may be one answer in what we've learned so far." Jeff looked at Anna who nodded in agreement. "You both experienced the same thing in the period between lives. You both said it was dark and you could hear a voice. Bill you could hear what it said clearly, but Kate you could only hear it mumble and said you didn't think you were supposed to be there. I know this might be a bit difficult to grasp, but since Lizzie allowed her life to be taken, it would have been a form of suicide. It may be why the voice wasn't clear to her."

"What does that mean?" Kate asked.

Jeff shook his head. "I'm not sure. I'm going to have to do a little checking on that. I'd like your permission to discuss this with one of our colleagues. It could be a touch of...some religions feel that suicide is a sin. The voice saying it's not the right time and you'll have to forgive, makes me wonder about the way Connor and Elizabeth died. Have either of you checked to see if there is any information about that fire?"

Both Kate and Bill said no.

"If you have time it may be a place to start. The Seattle Public Library should have newspapers from that period either on microfilm or they may have transferred it to the computer.

If you are interested in continuing, then I'd like you to do that."

"I can do it. Bill has his classes now and, other than moving to an new apartment, I have nothing else to work on," Kate said.

"Good." Jeff looked over at Anna. "Do you have anything to add at this time?"

"No," Anna replied. "I just want to remind you that you're still Kate and Bill, not Connor and Elizabeth."

"Do you think we are some kind of reincarnations of them?" Kate asked.

Anna looked at Jeff, who sat back in his chair. "It's hard to say flat out if that is the case. There are cases of residual memories people have, but usually those have to do with a haunting. I'm pretty certain this isn't a haunt."

"What does that mean?" Kate said and frowned.

"If you were being haunted by the spirits of Elizabeth and Connor, there would be more to report than just progressive dreams. You might hear voices when you're awake, or have things moved around your living spaces. Have either of you experienced anything like that?"

Kate and Bill shook their heads. "Okay, so we can say with some certainty that we were alive as other people and then reborn as us?" Bill squeezed Kate's hand and waited for an answer.

"I would give it about a seventy to eighty percent chance that it is probably reincarnation. There really aren't any references to correlate any findings we might get from the hypnosis. There are no cases reported of two people having the same progressive dreams. I'm afraid we're all walking into something very new here and I hope it doesn't put you off, but I feel excited to find out all we can from the research you do and a few more hypnosis sessions." Jeff smiled from his chair.

Bill sat up a little straighter. Kate let go of his hand, but he kept his arm around her shoulder. "I guess I'm glad someone is excited. Is there any side effects from hypnosis?" Kate asked. Bill saw an innocent look on her face and felt his skin tingle and turn warm.

"After this first session you might feel a little uneasy, but it will pass. Once we get to the bottom of Elizabeth and Connor's story, we can sort out what brought you together again. We might even find you were connected before them."

"Again?" Kate said. "Wait a minute, do you think that we might have been together before Lizzie and Connor? Do you think we've had other past lives together?"

"It's possible, but I think our focus should be just the one past life. And I think Jeff will agree with me," Anna said. Jeff nodded. "We'll do a little studying and have more information when you come back. Can we plan for next week?"

Bill and Kate said yes and rose from the chairs.

"If you have any questions or concerns that pop up during the week, please call us or send an email. Our answering service can find us easily during off hours, so don't worry about the time, okay?" Jeff said.

"I had about nine million questions a minute ago, but my brain just went blank," Kate said.

"Stop at the desk out front and schedule for next week. Tell Robin to allow two sessions," Jeff said as he shook Bill's hand.

They scheduled an appointment for the next week and made their way down to Bill's truck in silence.

Kate looked at him and said, "I need a beer. How 'bout you?"

"Sounds perfect."

They got into the truck and headed toward the freeway, not saying anything. Kate stared out the window and realized

Bill concentrated on the road. They stopped at a tavern called The Elbow Room, near the freeway. They sat in a corner booth on opposite sides and ordered beers. After their order was brought to them, the silence continued for some time. Kate gulped down half her beer. Bill polished his off in five minutes. The waitress came over and they ordered another round and a plate of steak fries.

Kate started to relax and looked at the bottom of her glass. "Bill, Elizabeth didn't die in the fall. When she realized Connor was dead, she put her head down and waited for the end." Tears welled up in her eyes and she looked across the table at him. "When I was in the hospital, I woke up and remembered everything. I heard my dad tell my mom that I was delirious. I was so knocked out with painkillers that I didn't really remember it until today. I guess that's why I hadn't mentioned it before. I'm sorry."

A tear fell onto his cheek and he wiped it off. He whispered, "I didn't know." He grabbed the napkin and beer, stood up and moved to Kate's side of the booth. He put his arm around her shoulder and Kate silently tried to slow down her emotions.

She rested her head against his shoulder. "Bill, why are we back? Do you think there is some reason to all of this?"

"I don't know. Hopefully we'll get that answered with Jeff and Anna. You really think it was us?"

She nodded and said, "Yes, I remember things now that feel as though they just happened yesterday."

"Yeah, I feel it stronger than ever."

"Jeff said we'd feel uneasy. I guess that's what I feel now."

They sat quietly for some time. When Kate looked at her watch it was eight o'clock in the evening. They left the tavern and headed back into Highwood.

145

Chapter Nineteen

Kate sat with Bill in the truck in his driveway, and continued to be wrapped up in thought. Kate sighed and was about to get out of the truck, but Bill stopped her.

"Why don't you come inside? I'll make some coffee. I may even have some decaf in the cupboard." He put his hand up to her cheek. "We should have more to eat than steak fries and I'm not ready to say goodnight."

"I suppose, we should talk about how we feel about the hypnosis today." She nodded and opened the truck door.

When they got into the house, Kate sat on the couch while Bill made a pot of coffee. After several minutes, he brought out two cups and handed one to her. He sat next to her on the couch and put his foot between her feet and his hand on her thigh.

She looked at him over the rim of her cup, and took a sip. "Bill, I'm not sure what to think about today. I feel really numb. That part about other prior lives might freak me out."

"Yeah, it's like we've been given proof that everything we remember is actually true, but my head is stuck. I'm not sure what to feel or think," he said and put his cup on the coffee table. "I think Jeff and Anna are honest, too. When you were hypnotized I could tell they weren't trying to scam us. I knew what you were going to say when they asked you certain questions."

"I watched them closely, too, but didn't see that they were trying to feed you any information. The questions were pretty straightforward." She put her hand on his arm. "Connor and Lizzie were so in love."

"That's the one thing I'm completely certain about. When you talked about putting your head down on my chest, waiting for the end..." He couldn't finish.

Kate put her cup next to his and turned to look at him. "Bill, I don't mean to change the subject, but your foot and hand ..."

He lifted his hand and moved his foot. "I'm sorry. I didn't mean to get touchy or invade your space."

"No, no. It's not bothering me. It's just..." She looked at him, started to laugh and stood up. She moved in front of him then spread her legs and straddled his lap. She ran her hands through his hair, and felt his hands on her waist. "It's just you're turning me on." She leaned toward him and lightly kissed his lips. "I know we were going to talk about today, but I'm afraid my mind is elsewhere at the moment. It has something to do with this couch and that kiss you gave me at Jeff and Anna's office...well, it's had me heated up for a while."

Bill sat up straighter and planted his mouth over hers. Their tongues twirled and touched. "What if I said I was subconsciously trying to seduce you?" She felt his hands move around her back and he pushed them under her bottom. "And that I don't think it's Connor's desire for Lizzie I feel, but my own attraction to you. When I first saw you, it was the Lizzie connection that made me want to be near you, but that's not how I feel now. I only see you, Kate." He looked up at her and kissed her chin.

She could hardly believe what Bill said. In the years that she and Henry were together, he'd never said anything so romantic. "Mr. Leary, that was the nicest thing I've heard in weeks. I'd like to thank you," she said, and leaned forward to kiss his cheek. She put one hand on his shoulder, and used her other to caress his eyebrow and jawline and then continued to lightly kiss his face.

"Kate, darling woman, in about one minute I'm not going to want to stop, but I won't force myself on you," he said, as he moved his hand under her shirt and kissed her neck.

The feel of his hand on the waist of her pants sent electricity through her body. "Bill, in case you hadn't noticed, I'm sitting on your lap of my own free will, for the very first time, if you don't count the wedding photos. In fact, I'm being kind of slutty. I'm sitting here thinking about taking off my top and undoing my bra, so you can have free access to my breasts. I'm thinking about you out of your clothes, and the feel of your skin on mine."

The words she'd just spoken seemed to take the long way-round to his brain. He stared at her and didn't take in a breath. She saw his lips start to curl into a smile. "Can I help you with the clothes off thing?"

She moved back on his thighs, put her hand on the front of his T-shirt, and pulled it up. While he slid the shirt off, she unbuttoned hers and let it slip off her shoulders. She unhooked her bra and it slid down her arms, then dropped it on the floor.

Kate grinned and looked down at him. "I knew you had a great chest. Now the pants are going to be the hard part. We're probably going to have to stand."

"Wait, don't get up yet." He ran his hands up her sides, and smiled at her chest. "You are so beautiful." His hands continued up and cupped her breasts.

"Thank you." The warmth from his hands caused her to sigh. She leaned forward and kissed his collarbone, as his fingers tickled and pinched her nipples. "Bill, sweetheart, I'm still being slutty. Can we get horizontal? This position is killing my hip."

He looked up at her again. "Of course. I'm not going to hurt you, am I?"

She gingerly moved a leg off the couch and stood up. He followed her and when he stood up straight, he leaned over and scooped up her legs. He held onto her back with his other arm. She was surprised by the sudden move and put her arm around his neck.

"Let me show you the way, darling woman," he whispered and walked toward the back of the house.

When they entered his bedroom, he laid her gently onto the bed. "Dreams do come true," he said, and smiled down at her. He lay down next to her and touched one of her breasts. He pinched the nipple between his fingers.

She felt it harden under his pressure and excitement coursed down her veins into her pelvis. "You've got that right. Dreams certainly do come true."

"Promise me one thing, Kate."

"What would that be?"

"If things get too intense and you start to feel pain, you'll stop me, no matter what. Okay? I don't want you trying to be tough like Lizzie."

"Deal."

***

He leaned over her chest and slipped the beaded nipple between his lips. He kissed and sucked on her breast, and caused her to squirm and moan. He moved back and forth between her breasts and let his hand wander down her good hip and thigh. His lips moved over her soft skin and lightly nibbled around her nipples. He loved the noises she made.

"Sweetheart, I've got to take my pants off. They're getting a little tight," he said, and laughed.

While he took off his pants, he watched as she maneuvered out of her own. When he realized what she was doing he tried to hurry, but lost his balance and landed sideways on the bed next to her. They both laughed.

"You did that same exact thing on our wedding night. Except you landed on the floor on your butt," she said, out of breath.

"Yeah, I think landing on the bed was much more comfortable."

She straightened herself on the bed, and put her head on a pillow. When his pants were off, he felt relieved; his penis had gotten quite hard.

Bill slid between her legs, nuzzled her neck, and brought his lips up to hers. What started as a light kiss, turned into a devouring, hot, tongue lashing and seemed to go on forever, he didn't want to stop.

He finally took his mouth from hers and moved down to her chest. He put his tongue and lips to work on her nipples again. She squeaked and moved her legs and feet down his buttocks and the back of his legs. His shaft pulsed in the V between her legs and he could feel her wet warmth.

***

Kate watched his head move around her chest and felt the heat race through her down to her toes. His tongue swirled in circles around the areola and he would lightly nip at her hard buds. She felt the pressure in her chest and an electric current travelled into her pelvis. She wanted him so bad, but didn't want him to stop on her breasts.

When he moved back up to her look in her eyes, he bit and licked her neck and chin. She could feel his penis lodge against her wet, warm folds. Her pelvis moved against it, and caused him to catch his breath.

"Miss Sullivan, you're causing me to have your slutty thoughts." He grinned down at her, and placed his arms on either side of her head. "I would love to freeze time right now. Your wet crotch is doing marvelous things for my blood pressure."

"You used the word *marvelous*, which makes me think you like?"

"Oh yes, ma'am. I like very much."

One of his hands moved down between them and she felt him put the head of his shaft to her opening. She closed her eyes and waited as he pushed his hard penis into her. She wrapped her legs around his waist and he slid another inch into her channel.

"Oh Bill, I never thought ..." she started to say something, but lost her train of thought as he began to pump in long slow strokes. She felt her muscles contract around him, and it seemed to make him go crazy.

"I don't want this to be over too soon. It's been a long time since I've made love to anyone," he said and slowed his pace. He looked down at her. "I'm not hurting you, right?"

She opened her eyes and grinned up at him. "No way. You are driving me insane, though. It makes me want to say something really naughty."

He dropped his jaw and looked shocked. "What are you thinking?"

"No, I can't say it," she said in a false, dramatic voice. "Lizzie would never say such a thing."

He pulled almost all the way out of her and then slammed back in. "Say it, darling woman." She shook her head. He repeated his move, and wiggled his hips side to side, which moved his penis around inside her. "Whisper it to me."

She put her hands up to his face, and ran her fingers through his hair. She grabbed handfuls and pulled his ear towards her mouth. "Do me hard, Mr. Leary."

"That's not so naughty." Bill laughed and slammed into her once more.

"I can't say the naughty word I'm thinking. I know you get the picture...oh, yes, you feel so incredible."

***

Bill growled deep in his chest and throat and let himself go. He lost track of how long he rammed his penis home, and suddenly, let go with a loud groan. He felt his semen pump into her. He couldn't remember such a feeling and was completely stunned at how relaxed he felt when the last drops released from the head of his shaft. He took a moment to catch his breath, then got up on an elbow and looked down at her.

"Kate, are you doing all right?" he asked, quietly.

"Yeah, I'm perfect."

He moved off of her, but kept a leg over hers, and put his hand on her belly. "You didn't have an orgasm. It makes me feel like I should have taken more time."

She opened her eyes and touched his lips with her fingers. "It's okay, sweet man. I'm not suffering."

"I can't have all the fun." He moved his hand down to the V between her legs and with a finger found her nub. "You're so warm. I may have to drive you a little more insane."

***

She moved her leg out from under his, as his finger danced and slid around her core. Tingling moved through-out the lower half of her body and she pressed her pelvis up to his hand. When she felt his head move and his lips encircle her nipple, she couldn't hold back and began to pant, and felt explosions of energy course through her pelvis. Lights flashed behind her eyelids as she tried to catch her breath. She put her hand over his, and let out a shout. "Oh, Lord above. Bill your fingers are wonderful."

They wrapped together in a tight hug and Bill put a blanket over them. They had teased each other for the better part of two weeks and she felt more than ready.

"You feel so good in my arms, Kate," he whispered, and ran his hand through her hair.

"You, too."

He turned on his side and propped his head in his hand. "You know, we were a little irresponsible. I do have condoms around here somewhere."

She opened her eyes. "I am on birth control pills, sweetie, and I sense you don't have any contagious diseases, which I don't have, either. Henry was the only other one."

"No, I have no diseases. If we'd been responsible we would have discussed this before, but, too late now," he said, and leaned over to kiss her chin.

"Yeah, you're right. We are adults and we should have been thinking, but, really, we had quite a day. I don't believe I was thinking clearly. I hope this doesn't make you think poorly of me."

"Sweetheart, you told me to do you hard. How could I think poorly of you?" He put his head on the pillow next to hers. "I don't think I could possibly have bad thoughts about you. I've wanted you since I first laid eyes on you in the garage and you're providing me with heaven right now. I can only think of you as an angel." He put his head back up and looked down at her. "Do you remember the night in the barn?"

"Do you mean the night three days before the wedding?" He nodded. "Yes, I do remember that dream very vividly. I told you I wanted reruns of that one."

"Lizzie never said anything, or didn't really have the chance to say anything about how she felt after it. Connor was nervous he'd scared or hurt her. Do you remember what her thinking was after that night?"

"It did bother her a little bit that she lost her virginity before being married. She saw him at the smithy the next day and felt excited and warm. She wondered about the warm feeling that came over her whenever she would look at him, even before the night in the barn. The night before the wedding, at the rehearsal dinner, she only wanted to go back to the barn. She didn't want to be in the church with her family and the preacher. She was a little naughty in her thinking, too. The preacher was explaining something about the service and she wasn't paying any attention to him. She wanted to ask Connor if the next time they mated if she could take all of her clothes off, instead of pulling her skirts up and having them wrapped around her waist."

Bill laughed. "What do you remember about the barn?"

"Oh...just about everything. I can even remember the way it felt. For being such a big, tall man, Connor was so gentle with her." Kate started to giggle. "When she first saw his penis, she wasn't sure how he was going to get it to fit into her. When it slid in, she was so surprised at how easy it was and it filled her with such joy." She glanced up at Bill and felt her face get warm. She was thankful the room was dark, since she knew she blushed. "This feels weird, discussing someone else making love. I feel like a peeping-tom, even though it was us."

"Yeah, but since it was us, then we shouldn't be embarrassed. Right?" Bill leaned over and kissed her cheek. "Connor was so worried after the barn. He kept trying to find a private moment to talk to her, but they were never able to be alone. When they sat on the porch in front of her parents' house, one of the sisters was always there, or Lizzie's father and mother. He thought about sneaking back over in the middle of the night and was going to throw pebbles at her window to wake her up, but finally decided that was a bad idea. If Lizzie's father found him traipsing around in the flower beds he might change his mind about letting the wild Irishman marry his daughter."

Bill kissed her again and put his head down on the pillow. They were quiet for a few minutes and then Kate moved around.

"Are we finished with serious discussions for now?" She pushed up and flattened him on the mattress. "All of the memories of the night in the barn are causing me to get warm again and I'd like to have you do what you just did some more. Lot's more, over and over..." She sucked in air, as his hand moved back down to her pelvis and his middle finger slid into her channel. "Oh yeah, more of that."

"Do you think Lizzie would have said something like that?" Bill laughed.

"Hush, and don't stop." Kate arched her back and sighed.

They made love late into the night. They laughed and talked. They touched and sighed, together. When Kate looked at the clock on his nightstand, it was after two in the morning. It surprised her, and when she told Bill the time, he changed her mind about driving home. He told her how he wanted to make breakfast for her in the morning and kissed her back into submission. She giggled and said she didn't feel tired at all. They got up and took a shower. He found a pair of sweatpants and T-shirt for her to wear to bed and when they crawled back under the sheets, it was all she could do to stay awake.

Chapter Twenty

Henry sat in his car, and watched the house. He'd followed Kate and the asshole all day and they'd finally come back to his house. Henry felt certain she would leave to go home, but as the time ticked by, her car stayed in the asshole's driveway.

He saw the lights go out in the front of the house and he waited for the front door to open, but it never happened. After fifteen minutes, he knew what was going on and felt anger rise from his gut up his back into his neck.

Henry fumed and after two hours, he started his car and pulled away from the curb. He made a decision and would put it into works the next day.

***

The next morning, Kate woke up and found Bill wrapped around her like a ribbon on a Christmas gift. One arm was under her pillow, the other under her arm pulled her back tight to his chest. One of his legs was over hers and she felt like a bear hugged her from behind. She could hear him breathe and it gave her a sense of peace and security. She pushed back to him and tried to feel more of his warmth.

She thought about their relationship that had grown so quickly in the last couple of weeks. Henry never made her feel such joy and she was so happy to be free of him. She hoped whatever developed between her and Bill would last. He was the sweetest man. She didn't think what she felt in her heart was from Lizzie and Connor. She held this feeling as her own.

Kate had a place to live and needed to move from the townhouse. Hopefully, when she and Bill went over to pack up the furniture Henry wouldn't be there. She didn't want any more arguments with him. Her dad helped out during the week, but since the move would be on the weekend, she doubted Henry would be at the office.

She managed to reluctantly crawl out of Bill's hold without waking him. She found her shirt and bra in the living room, put them under her arm, and headed to the bathroom. She got dressed and borrowed his comb to get the tangles out of her hair. When she came out of the bath, she found the bed empty, but could smell coffee.

Bill stood by the counter in his kitchen and broke eggs into a bowl. He wore his jeans, but that was all and looked wonderful.

"Good morning, Mr. Leary. I hope it's okay that I used your comb." she said, and stood in the doorway.

"Combs are free of charge, Miss Sullivan." He turned to her and smiled. "Good morning back. If it were still summer, I'd have some nice, sweet melons from my garden to feed you, but since its fall I'm afraid all I have are bananas."

"You have a garden? My, my, you are a man of many talents. Do you grow the bananas, too?" she teased. She walked to the back window and looked out. Sure enough, there were pots and rows in the soil. It looked as though it had been recently tilled.

He walked up behind her and wrapped his arms around her waist. "No, the bananas are grown at a place called Safeway. They do a very good job of it." He nuzzled her neck and sucked on an earlobe.

She laughed and turned around. She ran her hands up his arms to his neck and loved the feel of his skin. She gave him a quick kiss and pulled him close. She wanted more of his mouth.

157

"The tomatoes are my favorite. They're so sweet, it's like eating candy. I go out to pick them and usually end up bringing in about five. That's after I've munched handfuls," he said as he pulled back. "You have the most luscious lips. Would you like some coffee?"

It took a second for her to get her thoughts in line. "Yes, please, the coffee smells wonderful."

He poured her a cup and handed it to her. He turned back to the bowl of eggs, picked up a fork and started to stir. "I hope you don't mind scrambled."

"No, that's fine."

"So, what's on your schedule for today?"

"I need to head over to the townhouse one last time to finish packing, get some clothes to the donation shop, and confirm the rental truck. Hopefully, by this weekend, I'll be out of there and can start thinking about going back to work."

As Kate watched, he picked up the bowl, moved to the stove and poured the eggs into a frying pan. He adjusted the heat and looked at her. "I have a thought. Why don't you move into this house?"

"Bill, we've only known each other for a couple of weeks or so ..." she started.

"And, I feel I've known you for a lifetime." He walked up to her, took the cup from her hands and put his arms around her.

"Bill."

"I know and understand, but if you change your mind, the door's open to you. In fact," he reached into the front pocket of his jeans and pulled out a key. He put it into her hand. "That's the spare key, just in case. *Mi casa es su casa.*" He kissed her hand.

Kate took a step back, and looked up at him. "Are you an alien?"

"No." He laughed and went to the stove. "I just know a good thing when I see it and don't want to lose it."

"So, I'm a good thing?" She smiled.

"Oh, yes, ma'am. You're a very good thing. Have dinner with me here tonight. I'll cook and tell you all about the good things I see in you. I could even show you some of *my* better things." He looked over his shoulder and wiggled an eyebrow.

"It's getting warm in here. Are you sure you aren't from another planet?"

He turned back to the stove and stirred the eggs in the pan. "I'll be finished with class at noon. Why don't I meet you at this townhouse and see what I can do to help? Or, I'll meet you here, now that you have a key, and we can go together to the place." He turned around and leaned on the counter. "Why are you frowning? I don't want you to have another run-in with your ex. If I'm there, I could do my he-manly thing, to protect you."

Her frown turned into a smile and she bit her lip. She thought she might start to laugh. "I like your he-manly thing a lot, Mr. Leary." She put the key in her pocket and picked up her coffee cup taking a sip. "Do you need me to pick anything up for dinner tonight?"

"Let me think. Anything with lace is always welcome, or something that's form-fitting and skimpy is acceptable. Or one of those really tight tank tops that leaves nothing to the imagination. Oh, and maybe a toothbrush. I don't seem to have a spare," he said, and wiggled his eyebrows at her, again and turned back to the stove.

"A toothbrush I can do. I'll have to work on the lacy, form-fitting dinner outfit." She walked up behind him, put her hand on his tight bottom and pinched lightly.

"Miss Sullivan, you better behave with that hand of yours. I don't want to be rock hard on my drive to class today," Bill said, and chuckled.

She patted his behind. "Sorry, I'll behave." She walked to the dining room table and waited for breakfast.

***

Kate drove back to her parents' house, unable to keep from smiling. She couldn't stop thinking about Bill and their night of passion. It was a wonderful night to remember. She needed to get serious though and move to the new apartment. She hoped she could get everything accomplished in the next few days and then relax in Bill's arms.

When she pulled into the driveway at her parents' house, she saw Henry's beat-up Audi parked behind her mother's car. She felt her mom would be upset with her for staying at Bill's last night, but her dad knew who she was with and hopefully told her mom. She didn't look forward to a knock-down argument with her mom.

Kate turned her car off and got out. She felt as though she was headed into the house of doom. She opened the kitchen door and three sets of eyes turned to look at her.

"Where have you been?" her mother asked, sharply. "I've been worried all night about you. Do you know how inconsiderate it is not to call?"

"I have to agree with your mom, Kate. I wish you'd let us know when you aren't coming home," her father said.

"You've only been out of the hospital for two weeks, anything could have happened to you. We were almost ready to call the police," her mom said.

"I knew you were with Bill, but I don't have his phone number. You should have called us, sweetheart," her dad added.

Kate looked at Henry. "Go ahead and lay into me. It's your turn." He turned away from her and said nothing. "Great, not that it's anyone's business, but I did stay over at Bill's last night. We had a lot to talk about."

Henry huffed and sneered at her. "He's a mechanic, Kate. What could you have discussed? Cars? Getting your oil changed?"

Kate ignored him. "Dad, you do have my cell phone number. You could have called me."

"I tried, but someone's phone was turned off. You have messages." He looked up at her and frowned.

"Look, the time got away from us. Mom, Dad, I'm sorry you were worried, but I am twenty-six years old and no longer required by law to report in at a certain time. I don't have a curfew anymore. Bill and I talked until late and I was too tired to drive home. You should be really happy to know that Bill insisted it was too late to drive. He kept me off the road and I know you're not unhappy with me because I didn't wrap my newly repaired VW around a tree, right?" She started to turn out of the kitchen. "Lord, that didn't make any sense."

"Kate, wait a minute," her father said.

"Dad, please," she said from the doorway. "I was with Bill. I'm not hurt." When she started down the hall, she heard footsteps behind her. As she turned back around, she saw Henry come straight at her.

He grabbed her upper arms and pushed her hard against the wall. He leaned in close to her, and hissed, "I know what you did with him last night. I saw the lights go out."

She looked up at him. "You followed me again?" She tried to pull away from him.

"Yeah, I did. All the way up to Everett and back to the asshole's house. I should have known you were..."

Kate saw her father's hand wrap around Henry's upper arm. She looked at her dad and saw anger in his eyes. She wasn't sure if he was angry with her or Henry.

"Let her go," she heard her father say. He came up alongside of them and tightened his hand on Henry's arm. "Let her go now."

Henry let go and held both hands up, but continued to stare at her. "I don't know you anymore. How could you do this to us?"

"Let me refresh your memory, Henry. I'm the one whose mother you told that I drove the car during our accident, but, of course, you don't remember telling her that, do you? I'm the one who has asked you a million times to stop drinking, but you do it anyway. Henry, we're over. You need to get that through your thick skull." She started to move away from him, but stopped. "I'm going to finish packing my things up at the townhouse and I'll be out of there by this Saturday. If you want, I'll call first, to make sure you're not there." She didn't wait for an answer, went to her room, and slammed the door.

Chapter Twenty-One

Kate heard footsteps in the hallway that stopped at her door. There was a light knock and then the knob turned. Her mom walked into the room and closed the door. She watched as Kate changed her clothes.

"Your dad asked Henry to leave. Sweetheart, what did you mean when you said Henry didn't remember telling me you were driving?" She folded her arms in front of her. "He told me that. I remember."

Kate zipped up her pants, and went over to her laptop. She hit the Start button. "Well Mom, you shouldn't believe what comes out of Henry's mouth sometimes. He can lie with the best of them." She sat down on the bed to put her socks on and looked up at her mom. "Look, we're going our separate ways, and he's not adjusting to it very well. I was at the townhouse last week and he got really ugly and he's been following me." She started to put on her sneakers. "I've put up with his drinking for too long and I'm pretty fed up. Now he's telling lies to people I care for and I don't have time to deal with him anymore."

"Henry always seemed like a smart kid. I can't understand why this should be happening all of a sudden. I also didn't think the drinking was an ongoing problem." Kate's mom frowned.

"Job stress, maybe, or life, who knows? I've tried and tried to talk to him about it, but he doesn't see any problem. As far as he's concerned, there's nothing wrong."

"Hopefully, he sees now that there's a problem and will get some help. I'm sorry, sweetheart, that I didn't take you more seriously. I just didn't realize things had gotten so bad."

"Mom," Kate stood up and put her hands on her mother's arm. "You have no reason to be sorry. I haven't been completely honest with you and dad over the years about Henry. How could you expect to know what happened if I didn't say anything? You're not psychic. Bill and I are together right now and, yes, he works on cars and teaches, but he's a wonderful man." She went to her closet and pulled out a sweater.

"Sweetheart, this man, Bill, when will we get to meet him?" Her mother stopped and looked at her. "You were with him last night and you slept with him, didn't you?"

Kate almost started to laugh. "Yeah, I did and it was wonderful. When did you become so intuitive, Mom?"

"I'm not intuitive, I don't think. It just makes sense. I don't see how you've known this new man long enough to know he's the one. You've only been out of the hospital a couple of weeks and as far as I know you met him when you went to pick up your car."

"I've known him for a very long time." Kate looked down at her shoes.

"Since before the accident?"

"Yes. In a way."

"In a way? That sounds mysterious. Where does he live?"

"He has a house up in Highwood."

"He owns his house." She watched her daughter nod her head. "Well, that is something."

"Bill teaches at the community college up in Everett. He also is part owner of the garage where Dad takes the cars to be worked on. Mom, I think you'll like him." Kate looked up, directly into her mother's eyes.

"He's a mechanic, Kate. I'm not sure he deserves you."
Her mother huffed. "What a great catch," she said,
sarcastically.

"Yeah, Mom, he's a mechanic and I don't think I
deserve him. He's very smart and he cares about me." Kate
started to walk past her mother, who took hold of Kate's hand.

"Sweetheart, a mechanic? What are you thinking?
Henry has a good job, and he can support you and a family."

"Mom, doesn't it bother you in the least that Henry
lied to you and nearly got me killed? You still want me to be
with Henry, knowing all you do now?" Kate looked at her
aghast. "Bill is more than able to support a family and this
argument is ridiculous." She moved out of the room. "Is there
any coffee?"

Her mom followed her out to the kitchen. As they
entered, her father came in the back door.

"Ian, speak to your daughter. She's trying to ruin her
future," Maggie said to her husband.

"Honey, what are you going on about?" he asked, and
stood near Kate at the coffee pot.

"Your daughter is dating a mechanic." She crossed her
arms, and leaned on a hip.

Kate's dad looked at her. "You were with Bill all last
night like you told me, right?"

"Yep."

"I guess since I knew that, then I don't have a
problem." He looked at Kate's mom. "Maggie, he's a good
man and stable." Kate's dad shrugged his shoulders. "And the
hypnosis you were going to do the yesterday must have worn
you out. I'm glad you didn't drive late."

"Ian, I understand you know this man, but do you
really think he's a good catch for our daughter?" Kate's mom
asked.

"Yeah, he's done some work on our cars. He's part owner of the garage I take them to and he teaches. He's a good guy."

"Thanks, Dad."

"But don't you think she's being unwise to throw her relationship with Henry away for an auto mechanic?"

"Maggie, sweetheart, Henry just threatened my daughter for the second time in a week, so I really don't like him all that much right now and I think Kate is wise to move on. Besides, it really is none of our business." He put his arm around Kate's shoulders and gave her a squeeze. "She knows what she's doing."

Her mom looked at them both and clenched her hands into to fists. Kate felt a little guilty when she saw the slightly hurt look on her mother's face when she huffed out of the kitchen.

Her dad looked at her. "Bill seems like an okay guy and he is a good mechanic. Kate, are you sure?"

"Dad, what's your line about the only thing certain in life?"

"Death and taxes, and it's not my line."

"And Bill, Dad. I've never been so certain of anything in my life. He's really a decent, good man."

"Let's sit down for a minute. You do have a minute in your busy schedule?" He moved to the table, and pulled out a chair.

"You're being silly, Pop."

"Tell me about the hypnosis." He looked over his shoulder down the hall. "I was afraid your mom would pick up on what I said a minute ago. I guess I didn't say it loud enough. I didn't mean to let it slip."

Kate sat at the table opposite him and told him about her experiences the day before. Her father listened and asked a few questions, but he was mostly quiet, and let her continue uninterrupted.

After she finished, he asked, "What happens next?"

"Well, Bill and I have another appointment next week. Another 'session' as Jeff and Anna like to call it."

"Any idea what might occur?"

"None what-so-ever, Dad. It's a little unnerving, you know?"

Her dad nodded and asked, "Is there anything I can do to help?"

Kate smiled. "Keep Mom at bay as long as possible. She'll have kittens and never be able to understand any of this."

"I'll do my best, but you will have to tell her eventually. I did let the kittens out of the bag this morning. I didn't mean to mention the hypnosis. I think she was more worried about Bill being a mechanic. I have to admit, I find it a little hard to understand myself. It doesn't make sense scientifically. Reincarnation?" He looked at his daughter and smiled. "Remember, I'm on your side, but I feel like I'm reading one of the newspapers sold at the grocery checkout."

Kate continued to smile. "Tell me about it. I'm having a movie of the week moment." She heard footsteps behind her and turned around in her chair as her grandmother came into the kitchen.

"I'm sorry. I've been listening to your conversation from the hall. I think I have something you should see. Ian, when I moved in here, where did you put my boxes and steamer trunk?"

"They're in the attic, Mom," he answered. "We already found the pictures and marriage certificate."

"Grammy, what's going on?" Kate stood and went to her grandmother.

"You'll see," she said, as she turned toward the hallway. When Kate and her dad didn't move, Grammy turned back and ordered, "Well, let's go. Times a-wasting."

They followed her up the stairs. When the door to the attic opened, Kate's mom came up the stairs and stood behind them. She held an armful of laundry. "What's going on?" she asked. "Why are you going up there again?"

"Mom's looking for something." her dad answered.

"What?"

"I'm not sure. There's nothing to worry about, Maggie. We'll just be a minute." Kate's mom rolled her eyes and walked into the master bedroom.

They continued up to the attic.

"I want to look for my trunk. You know the one, Ian. That big brown monstrosity," Winnona said.

"Grammy, Dad already gave me the pictures from the wedding," Kate said, and hugged her grandmother's arm.

"I know, but there are some other things you might like to have." She smiled.

The trunk still sat in the open space. Her dad lifted the hinges and her grandmother stepped over to it. She looked around and then asked her son to help her take a large wooden tray out. She rummaged around the bottom of the trunk and pulled out a small and larger box.

"This is it. Come over to the table, Lizzie. Is there any more light in this room?" she asked her son. Kate's grandmother opened the smaller box and put her fingers into it. She pulled out a gold ring with an oval cut diamond. "This is your engagement ring, Lizzie. I bet you've wondered where it got off to." She smiled. "When I heard you talking about Elizabeth and Connor it reminded me of the pictures. Since you already have those things, I remembered the rest of it and think you should have it." She closed the flap and handed it to Kate.

Kate took the ring in the palm of her hand and paused. She looked at her grandmother and tilted her head. Her dad stood next to her. He put his hand on her shoulder and gave a light squeeze. Kate looked again at the ring and felt her throat tighten. She almost fainted. Her dad put his arm around her waist and she leaned against him. Kate put the ring on her left finger. It fit perfectly. She took it off again and held it up to the light. On the inside, she could see the words *Connor and Elizabeth Forever*. It looked like it was brand new, with no wear or scratches. She put it on her right finger.

Her grandmother then opened the second larger box. She pulled out a lace and satin dress, that Kate recognized immediately. It was Lizzie's wedding dress.

"Lizzie changed out of her dress at the church. Our mother took it home for her. I wore it the day I married your father, Ian, but it was always Lizzie's. She looked so beautiful that day. I didn't think of it until today, but I'm grateful now it wasn't damaged in the fire," Kate's grandmother said and patted Kate's arm. She then turned and found a chair to sit on. "Now it's back with the rightful owner. There's something else I remember from that time."

Kate and her dad waited in anticipation. "After the fire everyone was so distraught. My mother barely came out of her room. It was so quiet in the house, but sometimes you could hear her crying. I remember one day the sheriff came by to talk to my father. I was in the library, sitting in an alcove where I used to go to read. They came in and the sheriff said they thought that someone had set the fire on purpose. It was never proved and eventually it was forgotten. My sister Effie was never right in the head after that. She never married or settled down. I always wondered if she might know something about the fire, but never had the nerve to ask."

"Grammy, do you think she started the fire?" Kate asked.

"I don't know," she said.

Kate continued to look from the ring to the dress. She finally looked up at her dad. He mumbled, "How can this be?"

"I don't have a clue," was all Kate could think to say. "It's weird though, I remember Effie always followed them around. She had such a terrible crush on Connor and when the engagement was announced, Effie was furious. I do know I have to show this to Bill. Besides the pictures, this is more proof, in a way. Grammy, thank you so much for this gift. It means a lot."

"I hope it will help you find what it is you're searching for, dear."

Kate leaned over and kissed her cheek. She turned to her dad, "I'm not sure when I'll be back. I'll take it easy, I promise."

"If I can help in any way, you'll let me know?" he asked. "Hey sweetie, you are still planning on moving to the apartment this weekend?"

"Oh crap, yes. I was going to confirm the truck," Kate said and stopped at the stairs.

"I'll get the truck. Just let me know when and don't worry," he said. "Call me later with Bill's phone number, okay?"

"I will and thanks, Dad," Kate said as she headed out the attic door.

She made her way down the steps and walked straight down the hallway to the stairs that led down to the front of the house. She carried the dress box in her arms. It was a cold rainy day and she didn't stop to put on a coat or pick up her purse. She remembered to pull the spare key to Bill's house out of her other pants and put it in her pocket. She grabbed her keys and got to the car as quickly as she could. The cold woke her up as she drove to Highwood. She turned the heat up in the car.

Kate pulled into the driveway of Bill's house, and realized she probably should have gotten five speeding tickets she'd driven so fast. She remembered she ran a red light, too. Luck was on her side, as she had no driver's license or insurance card with her. She parked the car, pulled the keys out of the ignition and slammed the door.

When she got to Bill's door, she was out of breath. She put the key into the lock and opened it. She stepped into the quiet house and then remembered what time it was and that Bill was in class. For a moment, she felt at a loss. What should she do next?

Chapter Twenty-Two

Bill opened the front door. "Kate, are you here? I saw your car in the driveway." He put his papers and briefcase down on the table in the hall, just in time to get an armful of woman. He held her tightly. What's the matter?" Before he could get his senses under control, she backed away from him and put her right hand out. He kissed the back of her hand and looked into her eyes. There was a strange gleam in her eyes. "What?"

He felt her move a finger in his hand and looked down at the diamond and gold ring. His mouth dropped open. "What," he paused and looked at Kate. "Where did this come from?"

"My grandmother stored it up in the attic. When I got home I told my dad about yesterday. Grammy overheard everything and remembered the ring and wedding dress. They were in her steamer trunk up in the attic. I wanted you to see it and couldn't wait until whenever we were going to meet. So much for my lack of patience, right? It's more proof though, like the pictures were proof. This is the ring Connor gave Lizzie when he proposed. Look at the inscription. It looks brand new." She took the ring off and held it out to him.

Bill shut the door and turned back to Kate. "Why didn't you turn the heat up in here? You must be frozen."

"I wasn't really thinking. As I pulled into your driveway, I realized I didn't have my purse either. No driver's license." She crinkled her nose. "I got a little distracted."

Bill directed her to the couch, went to the wall switch and turned on the furnace. He took off his coat as the heat began to blow out of the floor vents. He came back into the living room and saw the wedding dress spread over his recliner. He went over to it and touched the lace. He remembered every inch of the dress.

"This is some sort of proof right?" Kate asked and pointed at the ring. "The really weird thing is, I remember Lizzie had a hard time getting the buttons undone in the hotel room. I remember that from the dream, but Grammy said she took off her dress at the church and my great-grandmother took it home. So, Lizzie wore a different dress, but I don't remember that."

He walked to the couch and sat. He took the ring from her and gave it a close inspection. "I remember this ring, that's for sure. There was a jeweler on California Street; I can't think what the name of it was, but I saved up as much as I could to pay for the inscription and the ring. I do remember the buttons, though. You said Delia was angry about them," he said and kissed the palm of her hand.

"Lord, I'd forgotten all about that. You almost spent your last penny on it." She took the ring from his finger and held it to the light. "Elizabeth and Connor Forever. It was so sweet. I remember I choked up when I read it the first time."

"Sweetheart, do you remember saying that during the hypnosis? That you thought I'd spent my last penny?"

She sat back and looked at Bill. She brought her hand up to his chin. "Connor?" she whispered. She pulled back and straightened her back. "It's weird, things...memories have gotten all tangled up for me. This must be that uneasy feeling that Jeff and Anna talked about. I remember that dress so well." She put her fingers through his and gripped his hand. "My grandmother said something else. She said that the sheriff thought the fire had been set on purpose. I'm definitely going to the library tomorrow. I've got to see if there is some record of the fire. I may even call the fire department to see if they have any records. Wait, no I'm not, I have to move tomorrow."

"That was a long time ago. Do you think they would have anything that old?"

"I can't even begin to guess." She shrugged her shoulders. "I suppose I could look on-line."

Bill picked up the folder with the pictures from the coffee table. He looked at the closer one of Connor and Lizzie. He could barely make out the ring. He closed the folder and put it back. He turned to Kate and took her hand. "Okay, here's a weird thought. Do you suppose we are being given a second chance? Maybe we weren't supposed to die when we did. It would make some sort of strange sense, don't you think? I mean I keep hearing that voice telling me it wasn't my time or whatever it said." He looked down at her hand. "I know this doesn't add in with...or maybe it does. Kate, I've been in love with you since I first saw you at the garage. It feels normal somehow."

She nodded. "I know how you feel. It feels right." She raised her eyebrows.

"Yeah, it does." He laughed. He kissed the back of her hand, again and smiled. "I keep wondering though..." He stopped, sat back on the couch and closed his eyes.

"Wonder what?"

He opened his eyes and looked at her. "I don't think I've ever been so afraid of something."

Kate remained silent and held his hand tightly.

"I keep thinking, what if we find out this feeling we have for one another isn't real? What if this desire I feel for you is really from Connor and Liz? Last night was so great, and I know deep down that you are mine, not theirs. I know that I've found you again and am the luckiest guy on the planet. It makes me crazy to think..."

Kate put her hand over his lips. "No, I don't believe that. I know we both have some turmoil right now, but I'm not going to think that what I'm feeling for you isn't ours. That it isn't real."

Bill looked at the dress and shook his head. "That dress is beautiful."

"You did say bring something lacy, but I'm not sure about the form-fitting. I'm not even sure I could get it on. Lizzie was a size or two smaller than me." She laughed. "I've looked at it for the last couple of hours. The things I remember."

"What kind of memories?"

"I remember my mother - I mean Lizzie's mother - doing all of that work by hand. She crocheted all of the lace and had no machine to do the work." She leaned against him. "I also remember all of the fittings. That makes me tired."

Bill chuckled and put his hand on her thigh. "Okay, I've got some tests to grade. Then we can head over to the townhouse and get it ready for tomorrow."

"Let's not do that. I don't want anything to spoil today. You grade papers. I noticed you have a computer. Does it work?" She sat up.

"Yes, it works."

"Does it have Internet access?"

"Of course it does. Doesn't everyone have Internet access?" Bill answered.

"Believe it or not, but not everyone has Internet. I actually know people who still hand write checks to pay their bills. I thought maybe you looked up stuff on the schools computer." She smiled. "No time like the present," she said and got up off the couch. She smiled and held her hand out. "Start it up Mr. Leary. I've got some things to look up."

Bill started up his computer on the desk in his bedroom. As it warmed up, he turned on the screen and fixed a pot of coffee. He then brought Kate a cup when it finished brewing. He watched over her shoulder as she searched for information and felt amazed at how fast read articles, trashed them and went on to the next. She went to the local newspaper websites and different search engines. She Googled and Binged. She found a brief article from a news history site. The title of it was *Broadview Inn at Alki Point Burns to Ground.* It was from 1912.

He read the short article along with her - *The Broadview Inn at Alki Point in West Seattle burned to the ground around midnight last evening. Sheriff John Evans says it looks as though the fire was arson, having found several empty kerosene cans in the alley beside the Inn. Five people died in the fire. The Inn is a complete loss.*

Bill stood up straight. "That's all it says? It seems like there should be more." He saw Kate look up at him. "What?"

"Aren't you supposed to be grading papers?" She grinned.

"Right. I have tests to grade. That's right; I want to get them done, so I can spend the whole weekend with you. I'll be at the dining room table." He left the bedroom and sat down at the kitchen table to grade the tests.

***

Kate sat up and stretched. She realized she'd been at the computer, in the same position, for two hours. She walked out to the main part of the house.

"Bill? Where are you?"

"Dining room," she heard him say. She walked through the kitchen noticed he'd put a pot of spaghetti noodles to boil on the stove.

He smiled at her when she came through the doorway. "I'm almost finished grading exams. Dinner will be ready in a bit. I just put the pasta on. I hope you like spaghetti."

"Did you make the sauce," she asked. She looked over her shoulder at the pots on the stove.

"What?" He continued to mark a paper with red ink.

176

"The sauce. Did you make it from the tomatoes in your garden?"

Bill grinned. "No, I did the manly thing and doctored up a jar of sauce. Why are you standing so far away from me?" He capped the pen and stood up.

"You were hard at work and I didn't think I should disturb you."

"Kate, your very existence disturbs me, but only in a very positive way. Meet me half way to the stove. I have to stir the sauce." He took a step toward the doorway and she met him step for step, and backed into the kitchen.

"So, you can cook. What else besides meatloaf, spaghetti and scrambled eggs?" She stood by the stove and watched him stir the sauce.

"Let me think. I'm pretty good at grilling - that's a manly thing by the way. I also made a Cajun meatloaf once. It was really good, but a pain in the butt to put together. I think it took me about four hours to get it mixed and in the oven." He checked the pasta and then turned and hugged her. "Now, isn't this better?"

"Better than what?"

He pulled back and looked at her with fake shock on his face. "Better than if I didn't have my arms wrapped around you, of course. Sheesh woman, I may have to kiss you back into shape."

"Oh, please, be gentle." She smiled and crinkled her nose. "When did you develop such a sense of humor?"

"I've always had a sense of humor," he said and leaned toward her. He gently licked her lips and when she parted them, he planted a kiss. When he pulled back, she frowned.

She backed away from him and felt confused. "I'm sorry, I don't remember you having quite the sense of humor you have now. The times were different and you didn't tease me so much," she said.

177

"Kate, I'm not following you. What are you talking about?"

She continued to move away from him and turned toward the back sliding door. "Connor didn't think manly things were important. He was manly, though. He took charge of everything." Kate turned back to him. "Did I tell you I was going to quit teaching?"

Kate felt the room grow warm and everything around her began to spin. She opened her eyes and found herself in a forest. She heard whispers come from the trees. She turned and tried to figure out where she was, when the whispers grew louder.

"Who are you? Do you know who you are?" they asked. The two questions were repeated over and over, sometimes fast and other times very slow.

She continued to turn and started to run through the trees. Up ahead, on what seemed to be a path, Kate saw someone peak at her from behind a pine. It was a woman, tall and slim, with long blonde hair. The breeze blew her hair around her face.

Kate stopped when she recognized the woman. "Lizzie, what do you want?" she shouted.

The woman smiled. "Do you know who you are?" she asked and then disappeared.

The trees and land around Kate began to spin and everything went black. She felt the ground fall out from under her feet and began to slide into the unknown.

***

Bill watched her and saw her eyes shake in their sockets. He realized Kate was not herself. "Sweetheart." He took her hand and pulled her toward him. "Can you hear me, Kate? Come back to me."

She looked at him and touched his lips. "You look so much like him, but...no, this is all wrong," she whispered and tears started to roll down her cheeks.

Bill put his hands on either side of her face. "Kate, listen to me. You're not Elizabeth. This is 2012. You need to remember where you belong."

He didn't think he made much sense, but was unsure what to do. He put his lips on hers, forced her mouth open, and pressed in firmly. He needed to wake Kate up. She moved her hands up his arms and put them around his neck, kissing him back. He looked into her eyes and couldn't figure out what was happening. As he watched, her eyes rolled up and she began to fall. He caught her and carried her to the couch. He set her down gently, then put a pillow under her head and waited. She felt very warm.

When she started to come back around, he went into the kitchen, turned off the stove and got a towel wet to try and cool her off. On his way back to the living room, he grabbed his cell phone from the table. He found her sitting up, with her head in her hands. She still cried. He sat next to her and put the cool towel on the back of her neck.

"Bill, what just happened?" she asked, quietly. "I feel like I just received really bad news."

"I'm not sure, babe. I thought you were having a seizure and was going to call 9-1-1 if you didn't come out of it. You said something about Connor not teasing and Lizzie quitting her job."

"I remember that." She looked at him. "Then I was in a forest and someone - no, it was Lizzie - kept asking me if I knew who I was."

"You saw Lizzie?"

"Yes, and it makes me feel really nervous."

179

"It's okay now. Do you feel all right? We can always go to the walk-in clinic to make sure," he said and took the towel off her neck.

Kate sat back on the couch and put her hands up to her face. "Bill, I can't stand this anymore. We've got to figure out what is happening. If I go into Lizzie mode with my mom around, she'll freak." She looked past his shoulder at the dining room table.

He'd put candles and a vase full of red roses on the table and forgotten all about them. He turned to see what she looked at. "The roses are for you, sweetheart."

"Oh God, I screwed up your romantic dinner."

"No, no. I turned the heat off under the pasta. It's okay," he said, and pulled her into his arms.

She cried and for what reason, he couldn't nail down to just one thing. The parapsychologists said there would be times when she and Bill would feel out of sorts. He tried to figure why she was suddenly so emotional. He supposed it had to do with Connor and Lizzie being dead, or her break up with Henry. She was still recovering from the accident. Why was she in a forest, seeing Lizzie?

"I want to get this sorted out in my brain, but I'm not making much headway." She wiped her eyes on the sleeve of her sweater. "I'm sorry, Bill. I should be happy. For once in my life I have someone to talk to about this past and present stuff and I don't have to feel like I'm losing my marbles. I found a place to live and, really, after a terrible car accident, I am alive. There's a gorgeous man sitting next to me, who bought me roses..." She cried harder.

"Plus your tall, he-man wants to wrestle with you at night, and he can actually boil water without burning the place to the ground." He stopped and realized what he'd just said. "That didn't come out the way I wanted it to. Listen to me," he said and took her hand. He kissed the palm. "We have a couple of things to celebrate tonight. You found an apartment and we found each other. I'm going to check the pasta. I don't want it to be mushy. Come, keep me company."

He stood up and held her hand. She stood up next to him and pulled him into a hug. "My he-man," she said into his shirt.

"I'm all yours. No more crying, okay? Or the pasta will get mushy."

She sniffed and dried her eyes again. "See, you do have a sense of humor." She leaned on his chest.

They went into the kitchen and he felt her watch him while he prepared their dinner.

"Bill, how would you feel about calling Jeff and Anna to see if we could move our next appointment up? After this weird moment I've just had, I don't think I want to wait a week."

"Okay. I'm all for it. My cell phone is on the table. By the time you're finished leaving them a message, dinner will be ready."

"I'll have to look the number up online. I left my phone at home."

"That's right, you didn't bring your purse and if you think I will let you drive yourself home with no license, think again." He smiled from the sink as the water drained from the pasta.

"I guess I better call my dad, too, and let him know I won't be back tonight. Hopefully, he can keep my mom from freaking out."

He watched her walk out to the dining room table and put her hand up to one of the roses. She leaned over and sniffed the flower, then picked up his phone. He walked up behind her and put his hands on her shoulders.

She turned and smiled at him. "Mr. Leary, I love you." She leaned against the table. "I love you right down to my toes. I know it's probably too soon, but..."

Bill shook his head and put his fingers over her lips. "No, it's not too soon. It's just the right time. I love you, too." He put his forehead against hers. "Make the call and I'll get dinner on the table."

Chapter Twenty-Three

The pasta was a little over-cooked, but Kate felt he'd done an exceptional job with dinner considering what happened.

She told him what she'd seen and then that everything went black. She put her elbow on the table and rested her chin in her hand. Out of the corner of her eye, she saw his hand come up and move her hair behind her ear. She reached up, grabbed his hand and put it to her cheek. "Bill, I'm not going nuts, am I?"

"No. I definitely don't think you're nuts."

"It's been an intense couple of weeks. Maybe everything just crashed on me all at once and my brain didn't know how to deal with it." She smiled and with her other hand touched one of the roses. "These are really beautiful. Thank you."

"You're welcome and I think you may be right. It's been crazy with the hypnosis, finding an apartment and everything else. I think we should take it easy tonight and get a good-night's sleep. Tomorrow is your big move and then you'll have to unpack. You'll need your energy."

"Very good logic, Mr. Leary. I like the way you think."

She helped him get the kitchen cleaned up and then they went for a walk, hand in hand, around his neighborhood for an hour. She looked for Henry's beat-up Audi, but never saw it parked anywhere near Bill's house. She hoped he'd decided to stop watching her and move-on.

The Sheridans returned Kate's call and arranged to meet them on Monday, just three days away. She'd get her move done and then she could focus more on the situation. She didn't like the possibility that she might have had a seizure.

She and Bill sat down to watch a movie, but about half way through it, Kate realized she couldn't keep her eyes open and said she needed some sleep. Bill stood, picked her up and carried her to the bedroom. She giggled and told him she wanted this kind of treatment at least a couple of nights a week. He put her on the bed and she slid off to change her clothes. She put on the sweats he'd given her early this morning, and snuggled under his sheets and comforter. She watched him slip his shoes off and pull his shirt off. He threw it in a corner and Kate decided he needed a dirty clothes hamper. He put a finger up and said he'd be back in one second. When she asked where he was going he told her that he needed to lock up the house, and switch off the lights. Her eyes were closed when he came back. She felt his warm body wrap around hers and he kissed her neck, whispering "goodnight" in her ear.

***

Kate woke up in the middle of the night and it took a few minutes to figure out where she was. She saw Bill stretched out beside her on the bed. She thought about waking him, but decided it could wait until the morning. She continued to look at him for a while longer and then felt her eyelids grow heavy, again. She thought that the coffee would keep her awake, but she yawned and drifted off to sleep.

Kate smelled smoke. A voice in her head screamed that it couldn't be possible, not again. Her eyes shot open and she shouted, "*Fire!*" She stood up so quickly she didn't realize her legs were tangled in the blanket. She tripped and landed on her behind. She pushed at the fabric from her legs and then stood, heading back to the living room. She found her way to a window at the front of the house and could see the smoke come in. When she looked out the window and saw the shadow of someone down in the alleyway, she put her hand on the glass. It was hot and she felt the palm of her hand blister. She watched the flames dance around the frame of the window and then the shadow she saw moved and ran down the alley out to the street.

Something took hold of her arms and shook her. She knew it was Connor and he kept saying to *"Wake up!"*

"Connor, we have to get out of here. The building's on fire!" she cried.

"Kate, wake up. It's just a dream." He continued to shake her gently.

When she heard him say the word 'dream,' she realized what happened. She turned back to the window and saw no smoke or flames and no alleyway. It was his front yard and she could see their cars parked in the driveway.

Bills wrapped his arms around her. "See? No fire. Are you waking up?"

"Oh, that was weird," was all she could say. She stared at the window and saw their reflections in the glass. She turned and put her arms around his waist, and said again, "That was very weird."

"Are you okay?" He rubbed the back of her neck.

She pulled back and looked at him. "Yes, well no, but I will be in a minute. I can still smell the smoke. It was so real. All I could think was not again. I can't lose you again."

Bill led Kate back into the bedroom and sat her down on the bed. He got her to lie down and then pulled the blanket over her and tucked it around her body.

"Go to sleep, sweetheart." He stood up and started to leave.

"Bill, where are you going?" she asked, scared.

"I'm just going to check around to make sure everything is okay."

"No." She sat up and held out her hand. "I don't want to be alone."

"Kate, I'll be right back," he said. "I just want to make sure I turned the furnace back."

"Okay." She lay back and pulled the blanket up to her chin. *After smelling that smoke...I'm almost afraid to go back to sleep,* she thought.

***

Bill walked into the hall and looked at the switch for the furnace. It was off. He checked the other rooms and the stove in the kitchen. Everything was off.

He went back to the bedroom and stretched out on the bed next to her. "Was it the same dream as before? The one when Lizzie and Connor died?" He turned on his side and put his hand on her stomach. "Hey, you're shaking. Come here," he said and pulled her into his arms. He could feel her movements and knew she must still be upset.

"It was and it wasn't the same dream," she said between sniffs. She put her head down on his chest and he ran his hand through her hair. "I want to listen to your heartbeat. It seems comforting, you know?" She pushed up on her elbow and looked down at him. "There was someone below the window well, outside of the inn. He stood in the alley. It was a shadow, but I keep thinking I'm missing something important." A tear ran down her cheek. "I can't figure it out."

Bill tried to dry her tears, but they kept flowing. "Don't push yourself, Kate. I know you're probably exhausted and I know I'm tired, but we'll get it figured out. We just need to give it more time. We'll see Anna and Jeff on Monday and see what they can make of all this."

"I know, but when I can't remember something it makes me hyper." She put her head back down. "Are you angry with me?"

"No, why would I be angry with you?" He squeezed her shoulders.

"When I came out of the hypnosis, you wouldn't look me in the eye and what you said...well, I can understand where you were coming from, but please don't be angry with me."

Bill pushed her onto her back and looked down at her. "My love, why didn't you get up and leave? You could have made it out and lived," he said and his accent changed to an Irish brogue.

"I couldn't go. There'd be nothing without you. You had become my world, Connor. I could not have existed without you at my side." She touched his face, and pulled her head up to kiss his lips.

Bill pressed down with his mouth and loved the feel of her lips. He wanted to kiss every inch of her, but knew she needed rest. He suddenly felt himself jerk and frowned.

"This is getting really annoying, I..." he said and sat up. "I feel like I have multiple personality disorder, just like you said." He looked back at Kate. He felt her hand on his back.

"Connor, we have an opportunity here. We can stay and be together. We could have the life we dreamt about," Kate said

Her hand slid up his back and Bill shook his head. He lay back beside her and looked into her eyes. "Kate, I know you're in there. Come back to me, sweetheart. Don't let Lizzie take over completely."

Kate started to answer him, but stopped. "Bill? I'm so confused. Why are they - or we - doing this? Are we haunted? I don't get it. What are we supposed to be doing?"

"What if we have Anna and Jeff try to talk directly to Connor and Lizzie? Maybe they could tell us what the purpose of all this is," he said. He turned back on his side and put his arm around her.

"That's a good idea. I want this to stop...oh, I don't know what I want." Kate wiped her eyes. "I do know what I want and I do know who I am. Bill?" She looked at him and stopped. "Don't look so surprised. I know I've fallen in love with you. It's very strong and I want to believe it's from me, but, at this point, who knows. I don't want to give you any false readings here. I think I know there's love in the mix for you. Please don't think I'm weird."

Bill propped his head up with his hand. "Hey. We've discussed this. You are not weird. I'm speaking as Connor, too." He moved his finger over her lips. "Did I mention how utterly seductive your lips are or that I can feel when you're looking at me? I really like it when you're watching me. Now I know for a fact, I'm one hundred percent certain it's me that feels this. I want to make love to you in the worst way, but this has been such a strange night. I won't force myself on you, Kate. That's one thing I can promise you. We have plenty of time for us to figure out what we feel for each other and what the future holds for us."

"You're trying to distract me, aren't you?"

"Did it work?" he asked.

"Yes," Kate said and rolled back into his arms.

He felt her force him to lie flat and put her head on his chest. He moved his hand through her hair. "Get some sleep, babe. I won't let anything bother you anymore tonight," he said and kissed the top of her head.

"I don't know if I'll be able to get good sleep, but I have to be alert for my move tomorrow. I'm not going to have anymore smoke dreams tonight. There...it's out. I said it. No more weird shadows in the alley," she said.

"You need to try and get some rest."

Kate laid back and he tucked the blanket around her. "I love you," she said.

"It feels right, right?" He turned off the light.

Kate shook her head yes. "It does feel right," she whispered.

Bill wrapped his arms around her and listened as her breathing grew deeper. He closed his eyes and silently prayed for peace.

Twenty-Four

When she woke up in the next day, Kate felt rested. She rolled onto her back, opened her eyes, yawned and rubbed her eyes. She realized she wasn't in her own bed and remembered the prior evening. She brought her hand up to her forehead and looked around the room and then down at her body.

"Right, I changed into sweats. What did I do with my clothes?" Kate mumbled.

She sat up and looked around the room. Her clothes were neatly folded on the back of a chair. She heard the sound of the shower and smelled coffee. She threw the blanket off, got off the bed and went out to the kitchen. She rinsed out her mouth in the sink and thought about brushing her hair, but realized she didn't have her purse.

"Great, just great, no brush. I'll have to borrow Bill's comb again." She ran her fingers through her hair and tried to get it to look decent. She saw a mirror hanging on the wall by the front door and went to check her appearance. When she felt she looked slightly presentable, she went back into the kitchen, poured a cup of coffee and sat down at the table.

The shower shut off and she smiled. Bill hummed a tune to himself. She heard him get out of the shower and he seemed to dress in record time. She sat at the dining table and listened to him in the bathroom. There was a light whirring sound that could only be an electric razor. She looked at her watch, which showed 7:00, so he must be getting ready for his class. For a minute she thought she should leave - he didn't need her in the way - but decided to wait.

After a few minutes, Bill appeared in the kitchen. He was dressed in jeans and a T-shirt. "Good morning." he said to Kate and poured himself a cup of coffee. "How are you feeling this morning, Miss Sullivan?"

She watched him sit across from her at the table. She saw a confused look on his face.

"You're frowning. What's the matter?" he asked.

"You're dressed a little relaxed for class, don't you think?"

"It's Saturday and a holiday. No classes today," he answered.

"Right, which holiday is that?" She laughed. "I know what day it is."

"And, you're moving today. I would say I'm dressed appropriately." He sipped his coffee.

"Oh, cripes. I'm supposed to pick up...no wait, Dad's picking up the truck," she said.

Bill handed her a cell phone. "Call your dad and tell him to wait an hour. We need to eat breakfast first."

She did what he said and watched him move around the kitchen as he cooked some bacon on the stove. She really enjoyed watching him move. She clicked the phone closed. "We have an hour." She stood, walked up behind him and put her hand around his waist.

"How'd you sleep finally?" he asked, as he turned the bacon over in the pan.

"Not too shabby and whoever it was that said things look better in the morning, deserves a pat on the back. I feel not as crazy as last night." She gave him a hug.

"Good. Why don't you have any coffee?"

"I do, it's on the table. How about I set the table for breakfast?" she asked and turned to the drawer that held the silverware. She pulled a couple of paper towels off a roll and went to work on the place settings.

"Hey there, ma'am, I'm the host. I'm supposed to serve you," he said and came up behind her as she placed the last fork.

"You were the host a week ago, but now you're just the guy who owns the house."

Bill's mouth dropped open. "Are you teasing me so early on a Saturday morning?"

"Sure, a little." She leaned against him, put her hand up and pinched his nose. Bill took her hand and kissed the palm.

"Thank you," he said and hugged her. "I want one kiss before we get terrible coffee mouth." He turned her around and gently caressed hers lips with his, which caused warmth to race into her pelvis.

When he pulled back smiling, she slowly opened her eyes. "Damn, you are really good at that. I'm sorry for the morning mouth." She sighed, and moved back to the kitchen table.

Bill laughed and went back to the stove. "I was going to cook eggs for breakfast unless you'd like something else. I have cereal or could make hot cakes."

"No, eggs are fine," she said. "We do need to get moving." She looked at the front windows of the house and frowned. She walked into the living room to the window and opened the curtains. She looked at the front yard and toward the road.

"There's plenty of time," Bill said.

"I'm going to have to head home first. I don't have my driver's license or debit card. I'll probably have to write a check to my new landlords. I'll have to remember to get that out of one of the boxes I packed." She continued to look out the window.

"What do you see out there?"

She looked over her shoulder and saw Bill in the kitchen doorway. He smiled and started toward her. "Nothing. I forgot to mention last night that Henry's been following me. He followed us to the doctor's office on Thursday. He was at my parents' house when I got home yesterday and I think I may have finally gotten it through his thick skull that we're over. I just wanted to check and make sure he wasn't out there."

"Sweetheart, do you think we need to worry about this?" Bill asked and walked up behind her.

She felt his chin on her shoulder and realized he looked out the window, too. "No. I think Henry's bark is worse than his bite." She looked up at him and smiled. "We do need to get moving, though."

Bill took her hand and walked her back to the table. He gently pushed her back into the chair. "There's plenty of time," he said, again. "As I said yesterday, if you think I'm letting you drive without your license, guess again. I'll take you home, you'll get your things and we'll go pack up your stuff. We need a good Northwest breakfast to build up our strength for the move."

Kate leaned back in the chair. "You're making this too easy, you know."

"Sorry." He smiled. "Just wait until I start to make it really hard."

"Hard?" She raised her eyebrows and bit her lip. "I might like that. How hard are you going to make it?"

"That is a secret, ma'am." He smiled at her and bowed. "Double meaning words and all." He went back into the kitchen and she heard him hum again.

"I don't have that much to move, Bill. A big Northwest breakfast might be too much."

"As long as the food is good, that's all that matters at the moment. For some strange reason, I'm starved this morning."

"May I be dismissed for a few minutes? I'd like to wash my face. And, can I borrow some toothpaste? I have morning mouth issues. And your comb? I don't have a brush."

"Sure, you know where the toothpaste is by the sink. There are wash rags under the sink, if you need one."

Kate left the table and went into the bathroom. She grabbed a washcloth from the cabinet under the sink, ran warm water and scrubbed her face. After she dried off, she combed her hair and then picked up the tube of toothpaste, squeezed some onto her finger and ran it around her teeth. When she finished rinsing her mouth, she stood up and saw Bill in the mirror. He leaned against the bathroom door with his arms crossed and a smile on his face.

"Why are you smiling, Mr. Leary?" Kate asked and wiped her mouth.

"I was wondering how you were going to use that toothpaste."

"Nervous were you?"

"Why would I be nervous?"

"Afraid I'd use your toothbrush since I forgot to bring one with the lace?" She turned to face him and smirked. Her left eyebrow raised and she giggled.

"You could have used my toothbrush. I'm not weird about that." He walked toward her and put his hand on her cheek. "I'm now going to do something and I hope it doesn't shock you." He leaned his head down and placed his lips on hers. He was so gentle; Kate started to lose her breath.

After a few seconds, he pulled back and ran his hand through her hair. "That was the first kiss after finger-brushing your teeth. Make a note of it. Also, it was the first kiss of what I hope will be many kisses, in the bathroom of my humble abode. Are you shocked?"

She smiled and shook her head. "It's a good thing you waited until I cleaned my teeth. Morning mouth can cause people to feel turned off really fast." She folded the towel and laid it on the counter by the sink.

"I've heard that. Now come with me, my dear. Breakfast is ready." He put his arm around her waist and they walked out of the bathroom. "Do you think we should take the picture of Connor and Lizzie with us? You could set them up at your new place."

"One of them and we'll leave the other one here for you."

***

After they finished breakfast, Bill drove Kate's car and by 8:30 they arrived at her parents' house. When they walked into the kitchen, she found her mom, dad and grandmother finishing up their breakfast. She could tell by the look on her mom's face that she wasn't happy. Kate decided it could only get worse before there was any chance of it getting better. She smiled, said good morning and introduced Bill to her family.

Her dad stood up from his chair and shook hands with Bill. They spoke about Kate's car and how it ran after the accident. Bill said he'd offered to buy it from her, but she wasn't interested.

Her grandmother looked at him closely. "Lizzie, you *did* find him. Connor it's been too long," Grammy said and got up from the table to give him a hug.

Kate thought Bill had charmed her grandmother. He tolerated her with smiles and hugs. Grammy kept calling him Connor. She took his hand and pulled him to the table, where he sat down next to her.

"Well, don't just sit there, Maggie. Get Connor a cup of coffee," her grandmother ordered.

"No, that's okay. I've had enough coffee this morning," Bill said to her mom.

When they sat down at the table with her family, it got silent for a few minutes. Her dad glanced at her and she tried to give him a determined look, but realized her determination was crumbling under her mom's stare. Kate thought, *there's no time like the present and the time has come to put the story on the table.* Her mom would have problems with it, but that was that. She started to say something, but her mom interrupted her.

"Henry called last night. He sounded very upset and spent the day looking for you. I think maybe you should call him and let him know you're all right," she said, flatly. "It wasn't hard to tell he'd been drinking."

"I'll call him later, Mom," Kate replied. "There are some things Bill and I need to tell you about and we have to get me moved. We don't want to worry you. We want you to know everything is okay."

Her grandmother continued to smile and stare at Bill. She looked at Kate and frowned, "Why shouldn't things be okay? I'd say they're working out fine." She leaned on Bill and reached for Kate's hand. "Lizzie, you've been given a second chance. You've got Connor back. Now everything will be fine." Her frown turned into a smile.

"Winnona, what are you talking about? That's Kate, my daughter, not your sister Elizabeth," her mom said caustically.

Kate squeezed her grandmother's hand. "You'd better let me explain, Grammy." She turned her head to look at her mom. "Do you remember when I was growing up, all the times I used to talk about my dreams? Do you remember that?"

"Yes. I remember. You stopped carrying on about that at some point."

"I stopped telling you about the dreams because you either made fun of me or told me I was a lazy daydreamer and wasting my life. Well, the dreams never stopped. They progressed and as I grew, so did the dreams." She looked at Bill. "I wasn't really dreaming though. I was remembering

196

another life. Bill was a part of that." She smiled at him. "Bill is a part of that, present tense."

Bill looked at Kate's mom. "All the years that Kate was dreaming, so was I. Only mine were from Connor's perspective."

Her mom's mouth was partly open. Kate waited a few seconds to see if her mom would respond, but she just closed her mouth and frowned.

Kate continued, "We went through regression hypnosis on Thursday and got a few answers. Not everything we've been looking for was answered, but it's a start. We're on the right track now. The one thing we do know for sure is that we were Elizabeth and Connor."

"Hypnosis?" her mom finally said. She looked at her husband and started to laugh. "This is unbelievable. Is Chip Coffee going to walk in now?"

"Maggie, just listen to what they have to tell us, please," Kate's dad said, calmly.

"Ian, our daughter is sitting here and telling us she used to be someone else. I suppose you lived another life?"

"It's called reincarnation, Mom." Kate knew this would happen. "Mom, how do you know about Chip Coffee?"

"Your father watches that science fiction channel at night. Don't change the subject just yet. Reincarnation?" Her mom shook her head. She looked back at her husband. "Ian, I think our daughter has gone a little nuts. I'm sure we can say it had something to do with the accident."

"Maggie, Kate hasn't gone nuts. She's told me about the dream for years."

"Told you? Why you?" her mom's voice rose.

"Because she knew I wouldn't make fun of her. She knew I would listen to her with an open mind."

197

"I see. So I have a closed mind." Kate's mom looked back at Bill and Kate. "This will go over big at dinner parties. My daughter, the reincarnated soul."

"Mom, who's going to tell anyone? I don't plan on saying anything to my friends, do you Bill?" she asked him.

"I don't really know anybody I'd feel comfortable enough to tell. They'd all make fun of me," he answered.

"So, unless you say something, Mom, no one else will know. But wait, we could go on the talk show circuit. I'm sure Ophra or Montel would love to hear about our story."

"Kate." Bill put his hand over hers as though he wanted her to stop.

"Or, we could write a book and sell the film rights. Let's see who should we get to play you Mom? Someone with a stiff upper lip would play you well, right? Maybe we could get Mary Tyler Moore. She played the part well in Ordinary People."

"That's not funny, Kate," her mom said quietly.

"No, it's not funny. Bill and I have spent our lives trying to figure out what these dreams are supposed to mean. We are finally getting some answers about who or what we need to thank for allowing us to be together again. It's a big mystery and all you can worry about is what your friends will think."

"Kate, this is not reality. Whatever fantasy world you've been living in all these years, it's finally come to a head," her mom said.

"Mom, this is reality. The dream that I've had with me all my life, was a reality. Elizabeth and Connor did exist. Ask Grammy. She was old enough to remember them and Lizzie was her sister. Ask Dad. They both saw the picture."

"What picture?"

Kate forgot that the picture was still out in her car. She turned to Bill. "It's out in the car; will you go get it, sweetheart?" He nodded, got up and left the room.

Kate's mom also got up and took her plate to the kitchen sink. "This is a remarkable way to start the day."

"Maggie, please, for once, just believe. Things in life aren't always black and white," Kate's dad said.

Bill came back into the kitchen and put the brown folder into Maggie's hand. She opened it and looked at the photo. "This proves nothing."

"Maggie, it proves everything," Grammy said forcefully. "I remember the day that photograph was taken. I was only ten or eleven years old, but I remember. Elizabeth and Connor were so in love and it was cut short. They died the same day. They're being given a second chance. A chance to forgive and have the life they deserved."

The silence in the room felt long and uncomfortable. Kate's mom put the folder on a counter top and started to wash dishes.

Something her grandmother said started to nag at Kate. "Grammy, what do you mean a chance to forgive?"

"She's just as loony as the rest of you," her mom said.

"Mom, please." Kate looked at her mother's back. She turned to her grandmother. "What do you mean?"

"It's all rather confusing."

"Why?"

"Last month when I went to visit Effie at the nursing home..." she started.

Kate interrupted. "Aunt Effie is still alive?"

"Yes. She's in a nursing home up north in Mount Vernon. I go monthly on the train to visit her."

"Why didn't you tell me?"

"Dear, you didn't ask. At least I don't think you asked. I would think you'd have known, she's been up there for several years. Anyway, last month when I saw her, Effie said she knew she would be forgiven. I asked her for what and she said I already knew. I couldn't figure it out, but it makes some sense now. With you and Connor back, I think she knew she would be forgiven for starting the fire. Or she knew who started the fire and why. Lizzie, I think she's ready to tell you what happened that night."

"Winnona, Kate is not Lizzie." Her mom turned from the sink with her hands dripping. "Can you hear yourselves? What you're saying makes no sense. It sounds crazy."

There was silence in the kitchen for a moment. Kate stood up from the table and walked toward her mom. She stopped and leaned against the counter. "Look, I know better than anyone that it makes no sense. Believe me, I really understand that and I'm still trying to figure out why it's happened this way. The one thing I do know for sure, deep in my heart, Mom, is that I was Lizzie in a prior life. Bill was Connor. I know that you'll have a hard time accepting it, but, Mom, I need to know why. I need to know," Kate said quietly. She turned to look at Bill. "We have to go to Mount Vernon."

"Tomorrow. You still have to move, today," he said.

"If we get everything moved by noon, we could go up this afternoon."

"Kate, if I remember correctly, you've got that big desk and couch to move, which will take some doing. I don't think we'll get it done by noon," her dad said. "Besides, aren't you going to unpack?"

"We could try, couldn't we?" Kate answered.

Chapter Twenty-Five

Henry sat in his car, and waited. It was a cold, foggy morning and he'd finished a hot cup of coffee about an hour ago. Now, he thought about turning the car on to get the heater started. He was frozen.

He waited patiently for Jack's Gun and Hunting Supplies to open their doors. He'd once heard from someone that the last fifteen minutes could be the longest. It was true; he kept looking at his watch to make sure it worked.

He'd made his decision about what he needed to do - what he should have done a long time ago - and was ready to put everything into motion. He'd hoped the fire would kill only him, but it took her, too. He had to convince Kate to stay with him.

He wanted her for eternity and there was only one way to make her see the truth of the situation. He needed to get rid of the intruder. Too long ago, he'd let her slip away and this time he would make her see. He offered more than that stupid, too tall asshole. It seemed fitting that he used to shoe horses and now he was an auto mechanic. One horse to another seemed to fit.

Henry saw a bright neon sign light up in the gun shop's window that showed it was open. He got out of his car and walked across the gravel parking lot. As he opened the door, the pungent smell of gun oil and metal hit his nose. He walked to a glass-fronted case and looked down at the handguns.

A short, overweight sales clerk with a dark mane of hair and scraggly beard slid around from behind the case and approached Henry.

"Good morning, sir. How can I help you?" the clerk asked. A stained name tag pinned on the guy's shirt gave his name as Ted.

"I'm looking for a handgun. Something I can protect myself with," Henry said as he looked into the case.

"Do you want something concealable or will you carry it in view?"

"I'll probably have it in the car. My job takes me to some bad neighborhoods," Henry lied. He saw the look on Ted's face change and thought, *the idiot probably thinks I'm a process server or bill collector.*

"I see." Ted leaned over and opened one of the cabinets. "We'll want to find something for you that has a comfortable grip and is easy for you to use. The higher caliber guns can have some kick back and I don't think you'll need anything that powerful." Ted brought out two different types and laid them on the counter.

Henry tried holding several of the pieces and finally found one that fit nicely in the palm of his hand. It was a Smith and Wesson revolver and it felt great. Ted gave him all kinds of information about the gun, but Henry didn't listen. It was the answer to all his problems.

Henry smiled. "This is perfect. I'll take it and a box of bullets."

"Great. I'll need for you to fill out some paperwork, sir." The clerk turned and produced a stack of papers.

"Why?" Henry frowned.

"The law requires a waiting period that can be up to thirty days. They'll want to do a background check on you."

Henry stared at the guy. Somewhere in the back of his head he knew this might happen. "I don't have thirty days. Maybe you know someone. I have cash." He saw Ted's forehead crease and figured the wheels had just fired up in the guy's fat brain.

"Yeah I might know someone, but..." Ted paused.

"But?" Henry watched him closely.

"How do I know you're not with the ATF?"

"I guess you don't. You'll just have to take my word for it." Henry smiled, again.

"I'm sorry, sir. Rules are rules. You'll have to fill out the forms or take your business elsewhere." Ted put the guns back into the case and closed it. He straightened up and gave Henry a firm look.

"Fine. It's your loss." Henry turned and left the shop.

It took three more tries before he found an illegal dealer who turned a blind eye to the background check. He got a six shot .38 caliber snub-nose. Now all he needed to do was find his target and he'd be home free.

***

The move took longer than Kate wanted. They finished unpacking the truck around four in the afternoon. Bill knew she pushed as hard as she could, but in the end she was worn out. With everything that happened the day before, the move, and then being told that Effie was still alive running through his brain all day, he was worn out, too. Her father took them out for an early dinner, and then dropped them back at Kate's new home.

Kate went into the kitchen to unpack boxes, so Bill went into the bedroom to set up her bed. The frame went together easily and he plopped the box spring and mattress on top. He looked around the room, and wondered where a box with sheets might be. He shouted out to Kate "Sheets? Where might I find sheets?"

"They're here somewhere," she answered. He heard her walk into the living room. She must be trying to find the box they were packed in. "You know, we could have gone up to Mount Vernon today."

Bill walked out of the bedroom and stood in the hall. "Oh, we're just putting off until tomorrow what we could have done today. That cliché." He smiled. "We don't see Anna and Jeff until Monday afternoon. Tomorrow is Sunday. We could sleep in and head up mid-morning."

"Bill, you're being flip," she said, as she pulled a set of sheets out of a box and threw them to him. He watched her turn and walk back into the kitchen. He followed her.

"Do you get testy when you're tired?" he asked lightly.

Kate sighed, leaned against a counter and looked at him. "Sorry, I am getting testy. Thank you for setting up the bed." She looked at her hands and rubbed them together. "After all these years of wondering, we have the possibility of an answer. I feel like we've wasted a whole day. I know, I have a problem with patience sometimes, but I want to know what Aunt Effie can tell us."

"We'll find out. Less than twenty-four hours and we'll be on our way."

"We could have known today." She looked at him.

Bill sensed something in Kate's attitude that made him love her more. "I know you're impatient, but are you a little scared, too?"

Kate tilted her head. "I wouldn't say 'scared'. A little nervous I'll admit to, but not scared." She began to open another box.

Bill turned back to the bedroom. "I think I'll make the bed."

"Bill, wait a minute." He turned back to her. "Look, you've done enough. You don't have to make the bed. I should get you back to your house. It's been a long day. I'm sure you want some peace and quiet. Maybe get cleaned up. I'm sure you have some work to do for your Monday class, too."

He hugged the sheets. "You're trying to get rid of me?"

"No." She looked up. "I just thought you might want to get a decent night's rest after you slept next to personality numbers two and three last night."

"You're getting testy again." He smiled at her. Bill suddenly wanted to say three very important words to her, but didn't think she was in the right frame of mind.

She closed her eyes and grunted. "I'm not getting testy. I've just stated facts."

"Kate, is there something on your mind that you want to talk about, but aren't sure how to start?" he asked.

She looked up at him. He didn't like the frown that appeared on her face.

"Let's sit down a minute. I need to get off my feet," she said.

They walked out to the living room and sat on her couch. He could tell there was something on her mind and it seemed to upset her. He hoped she felt comfortable enough with him to bring it up.

"Okay, here goes. For some crazy reason it annoys me that you can tell something is bothering me. That's the first thing," she said. "What happens if we do or don't get the answers we're looking for?"

He thought about her statements and wanted to say the right things. "On the first thing, I'm sorry it annoys you and I'll try not to notice when you've got something on your mind. Now, what do you mean, 'not getting the answers'?"

"Apology accepted. What if we find out the reason we were brought back? What if tomorrow, Aunt Effie tells us some earth-shattering reason. What then? What if Aunt Effie says nothing meaningful tomorrow? How long do we continue hypnosis? What do we do if there is no purpose and we're just here with someone else's memories? Then what?" She looked at him, and her eyes didn't blink.

"That's a lot of *what if's*," he said. "We don't know what tomorrow will bring. We just have to wait and see."

"Okay, let me ask another question. I have very serious feelings for you. We said, last night, that we're falling in love. What if all of these feelings are just the memories? Something brought with us from the past? Is it really us feeling it or just the memory of the moment?"

"I can see you've thought hard about this. I may have a difficult time not noticing when you're bothered by a conclusion. Sorry," he said. "I'm pretty sure it was you who said I love you last night."

"Yeah, and I feel hyper about it, too." She started to laugh. "I know it's crazy, but I started to wonder about it this morning. What if we get all the answers and suddenly find out we can't stand one another? What if it was Lizzie and Connor who were in love and not us?"

"Hmm." Bill leaned back on the couch and closed his eyes. He thought for a minute and could understand what she expressed. She'd had that dream or seizure, or whatever, with someone asking *if she knew who she was*. It must have upset her more than he'd originally thought.

"Are you falling to sleep?" he heard her ask.

"No, just thinking." He opened his eyes and looked at her. "I thought about that and we've superficially discussed it. I don't think that's the way it's going to work out though."

"You don't? Why?"

"Well, we're both pretty strong-minded people. We know ourselves. We've had a little bit of a hiccup with all this, but we both are pretty level-headed. Do you think what you feel aren't really your own feelings?"

"No," she said.

"You almost sound disappointed."

"I'm not disappointed. I don't know what I am. You say I'm level-headed, but when it comes to the dream and the past I'm not sure what I'm supposed to feel."

"There's no supposed to be in this, you know?" He reached up and touched her cheek. "We'll both get it figured out. If we do or don't find out anything tomorrow or next week or the week after that, it won't matter much to me. I know I love you. No one could tell me anything different at this point." He smiled. "So why are you trying to get rid of me?"

"I'm not trying to get rid of you." She looked uncomfortable. "It's just that you were talking about making the bed and..."

"Ah, the heart of the matter." He smiled. "Sweetheart, we have slept together."

"No, that's not it and you know it. Yes, we've slept together and we've done even more than just sleep. It's just, there's a couple of people upstairs and I'm not sure how soundproof the walls are. If I start moaning too loudly...well, you get the picture."

"Got it. This couch feels very comfortable on my behind as I sit here. I think if I need to sleep on this couch, it would work just fine. In fact, the couch will work just fine until we're back at my place, with some privacy. As long as you don't make me wait until we're married, though."

"Married?" She pressed her lips together. "Aha! There's another thing I've tossed around. You asked a few minutes ago if I was scared. Well, what if we make love again and a fire really does start? Or, what if we get married and another fire starts?"

"Kate, do you always worry this much?'

"No, it's all a part of that wondering thing. Last night in your room I could have sworn I smelled smoke. That was real.

When I smelled it, the first thing I thought was, *not again*. Do you think I'm being paranoid?"

"No, not paranoid. I do think you need to turn your brain off for a bit. What is your heart telling you?"

"I'm not listening to my heart."

"Why not? Sometimes the heart has a better way of looking at things than the brain does. The brain gets too suspicious and spends too much time trying to figure out what's going to happen next. How about we give your impatience a rest? Take in a breath and we'll see what happens tomorrow when it happens. The thing I'm the most thankful for is that I won't have to face it alone. I know you'll be right there with me. We can do this."

"I like how you sound so sure."

"Now, I'm sure I'm going to make the bed. You need some rest. First, you can show me that toothpaste on the finger trick. I've never done that before."

Bill made the bed. Kate got most of the kitchen unpacked. He helped break down boxes and stacked them in a corner by the front door. It was after nine o'clock and he knew Kate was tired. He walked out of the bedroom and watched as she looked around the kitchen. He went into the living room and saw a six-foot tall bookshelf that she said she wanted against a different wall. He walked over, lifted the case and moved it to the wall she had pointed out. He tapped the top shelf and thought that was enough for one day. He saw the lights go out in the kitchen and saw her move around the corner.

"You might want to just lean that against the wall. It will have to be screwed to a stud and I'm not sure where the screwdriver is," she said.

"Why does it have to be screwed to the wall?" he asked.

"It's pretty tall. If Seattle ever does have the great earthquake the prognosticators predict, that thing will crash over. It'll make me feel safer if it's attached." She smiled at him. "Are you sure you don't want me to drive you home tonight?"

"No, it's too late and you're too tired. We'll stop by there tomorrow for breakfast before going to Mount Vernon," he said, calmly.

"Wow, that's right. I don't even have any coffee," she said, yawning. "I'm getting ready for bed. I think I have a surprise for you."

"Yeah? What?"

Kate smiled broader and went down the hall to look in the boxes lined up along the wall. He followed her and watched her bend over and open one. She moved things around and pulled out a new toothbrush still in its plastic package. "No finger brushing for you." She handed him the toothbrush.

"Now I'm getting worried. You stock toothbrushes?"

"They give them to you when you go to the dentist to get your teeth cleaned. I've got a couple extra I can part with." She moved toward him and gave him a light kiss. "Now, you've experienced bad breath."

He smiled. "I can deal with it."

Kate hooked her finger on his T-shirt and started to pull him toward the bedroom. "Come to bed, Mr. Leary and promise not to make me moan too loud."

"What about the couch? My back was really looking forward to it."

"You're looking much too hot and I'm having a second wind all of a sudden." She arched her eyebrows. "I want to be naughty for a little bit." She pulled him past the door and closed it. She sat on the edge of the bed and opened her legs, moving him between them.

He felt her fingers slide his belt out of the loop and unhook it. He put his hands in her hair and tipped her face up.

He leaned over and brushed her lips, kissing around the sides. Her hands moved up to his waist and pulled him down to his knees. He moved his hands around her back and hugged tight.

He looked up at her beautiful blue eyes. "Kate, you don't have to respond, but I know right now, at this moment, I want you with me the rest of my life. I never want us to be apart."

He heard her sigh. "I love you, Bill."

Chapter Twenty-Six

When she opened her eyes, the room looked dark and strange. She didn't recognize the place and the bed felt wrong. She rolled onto her back, looked up at the ceiling and tried to figure out where she was. She looked at the man lying next to her. He looked so peaceful and breathed deeply. She realized this was the new place and she should feel happy.

She sat up on the bed and threw the covers off her to the side. She put her feet on the floor and saw she wore very strange stockings. They only covered her feet and ankles.

She walked out of the room in the darkness. There was light that came from a lamp outside the window and it made it possible for her to see the stacks of boxes lined up in the hallway. She found a room that resembled a kitchen. It seemed so strange to have a stove which didn't require wood or matches. She stopped and looked at the sink. It amazed her that if she turned a shiny knob water would spit out of the pipe. She stared at it for a few seconds then twisted around and moved out of the room.

She went to the door and managed to get it open. She went up the steps to the yard outside of this strange house. She looked up at the night sky and saw a crescent moon and some stars. It was chilly, but the air felt good and smelled fresh. There weren't as many stars in the night sky as she remembered.

Hands started to move around her waist and she smelled her husband's scent. She leaned back and let his arms enfold her.

"Mmmm...hello husband."

211

"What are you doing up, my lass?" his voice said in her ear. His hand moved up the front of the nightshirt she wore and tickled her stomach.

"Oh, thinking of dancing with you in the moonlight. This is a lovely area to waltz, don't you think?"

His hands turned her around and pulled her to him. His lips covered hers and pressed down gently until she opened her mouth and gave him entrance. His kiss became fiercer and caused her to lose her breath. He sucked her tongue and lips, and bit her chin. She put her hands up into his hair and held onto him. He grabbed at her behind and pulled her up so her legs wrapped around his waist.

"It was so strange to see you in slacks. I'm not sure I'll be liken it, my love," he said. He slowly moved to the side of the house and pressed her against it. His hands were warm as they moved along her thighs.

"Kate wears very strange undergarments, too," she said and kissed his neck.

"May I see them?" he asked and grinned.

"Of course, you may, my darling. We are married after all." She smiled and pushed him back and slowly raised the front of the nightshirt.

Her husband's breath caught as he looked at her lacy panties. His hand moved down and touched her stomach above the top of the lace. "Lass, it is strange, but beautiful all the same. Are your nipples hard for me?"

"As you are hard for me, my love." She smiled and felt his member press against the junction between her legs. "Bill wears no night wear to sleep, just as you did on our wedding night. It would seem you are again naked."

His fingers moved the nightshirt up and she pulled it over her head. He put his head down, kissed between her breasts and bit the soft skin lightly. He moved to one and took the bead between his lips. He pressed his tongue down and when he lightly bit it, he was rewarded. She sucked in air and wrapped her arms around his head. She felt a tingling in her body she'd never felt before and thought she could come to love it.

"Oh my lass, I want your body so desperately," he said against her chest.

"Dare we use their bodies in such a way?" she asked and felt heat run through her as he twisted her hard nipple with his fingers.

"They are attracted to one another. They've already coupled, it is only a matter of time before they too marry," he said and straightened his back. He looked into her eyes. "I have been away from you too many nights."

"They aren't ours. We have to respect them." She quickly kissed his lips. She glanced toward the street and saw a shadow move by a row of bushes. She pulled up to hug him tight. "My love, there's someone watching us," she whispered.

He let go of her breast and looked over his shoulder.

"He's watching us now," she hissed, as he slowly lowered her to the sidewalk.

"Better put your night dress back on." He looked down at her and blocked her nakedness from whoever might be out there. "Where did you see him?" he asked as she pulled the gown over her head.

"By that row of bushes across the road, he's crouched down by the second one from the left."

"I see him." He put his forehead against hers. "I want you to go back into the house, my love."

"What are you going to do?" she asked and held onto him.

"I just want to find out what he wants."

"You should put on some clothes, don't you agree? He might possibly hurt you." She looked up at him. "I think we

213

should call the police first," she said and shook her head. She saw Bill do the same thing.

He finally looked at her, took her hand and led her back into the basement apartment. Bill picked up his cell phone and dialed 9-1-1.

The police came and checked around the house and the yard across the street. They found footprints in the dirt around the bushes, but whoever hid there was gone. The officers felt they didn't need to worry about it, but if the guy came back to be sure to call.

Bill held onto to Kate as the police cruiser pulled away. "I don't feel like I should plan on leaving you alone anytime soon," he said and looked down at her. "I think we need to discuss what just happened."

"You're right about that." He took her hand and led her back into her new home. "What did just happen?" she asked as she locked the door and turned a light on in the hallway.

They moved back into the bedroom and sat down on the bed. When he saw she sat away he frowned and moved to the middle, next to her. He put the blanket from her bed over their legs.

"Bill, I knew what was happening, but didn't seem...I mean, I knew what I wanted and...I was awake, but..." She stopped and put her hands on either side of her face. "I'm confused."

"Do you remember the day Henry pushed you against the car and bruised your shoulder?" he asked.

"Sure," she said and looked at him.

"Do you remember turning to me and saying 'he was very cruel to her'?" He waited for a response, but she only shook her head. "I didn't think anything about it then, but I wonder if maybe we're being haunted by Connor and Lizzie. I mean, oh man...I don't know what I mean. I said a day or so ago I feel like I have multiple personalities, but now I wonder if we're possessed."

"Bill, I'm not sure I like that one bit," she said and frowned. "I hope this doesn't mean we need a group of ghost hunters."

"Same here. Monday, when we see Jeff and Anna, we need to get this sorted out once and for all. I really feel out of touch."

"That's a good idea. Bill, I'm sorry I was so flaky about the sheets and everything earlier. I'm really glad you stayed tonight. I just feel as though I'm going in fifteen different directions right now." She looked up at him.

He laughed. "After our little tryst out at the side of the house, I'm right there with you and that includes our activities earlier in your bedroom. I even sounded like I was from Ireland. Who was making love to whom?"

She leaned into him. "That's a good question. I was afraid to bring it up."

Chapter Twenty-Seven

Bill and Kate got up the next morning and, after he ran to the convenience store to get them coffee, they left her apartment to get breakfast. She apologized for not having thought of going to the grocery, but he wouldn't hear of it. There were so many things on their minds yesterday, who could have worried about food? After breakfast they went back to Bill's house in Highwood, where he got cleaned up and changed his clothes.

Kate called her parents' house to get the address of the nursing home in Mount Vernon. She didn't think they'd have any problem finding it. Her dad said that they could visit from ten o'clock to five on Sundays, according to Grammy. He told her that her mom, Grammy and he would meet them there. Kate protested, but he said he didn't want them to do it alone. He also thought it would be good for her mom. If Effie gave any information that would get them closer to an answer, her mom might be more inclined to believe in the dream.

It would take at least an hour to get to Mount Vernon. They took Kate's car. She pulled a map out of the glove box and, while she maneuvered the car onto the freeway, Bill looked at it and told her that he thought he could figure out where they were supposed to go.

They made it to Mount Vernon a little before ten o'clock and, after a couple of wrong turns, found the nursing home and parked the car. They sat in the car for a few minutes.

"How do you think we should begin this?" Kate asked.

Bill looked out the front window. "I'm not sure," he answered. "Take it one step at a time?"

"Yeah, I hope we don't give her a heart attack."

He looked at her. "Maybe we should go in one at a time."

"Maybe." Kate looked in the rearview mirror and saw her father's car pull into a parking space behind them. She pulled the keys out of the ignition and said, "They're here. Maybe Grammy should go first. She could explain the situation."

They got out of the car and slowly made their way to the front entrance of the building. Kate's mom, dad and grandmother followed them into the main reception area. Grammy walked up to the front desk.

"Good morning, Mrs. Sullivan. How are you today?" the receptionist asked.

"I'm just fine, Sarah, thank you. We're going to see my sister," she answered.

"All of you?"

"Yes, this is my son and his wife. Over there is my granddaughter and her boyfriend."

Bill and Kate smiled at each other and waved at the young woman. Kate felt a little relieved that Grammy knew who she was this morning.

"Well, how about you sign in for everyone, Mrs. Sullivan? That should work out fine." The woman smiled at Grammy.

After she'd signed them in, they followed Grammy down a hallway. The doors of many rooms were opened and somewhere down another hallway they could hear someone yelling. Grammy turned to the group and whispered, "That's probably Mrs. Howard. She has Alzheimer's. Can't remember where she is most of the time."

They turned another corner and came to room 104. The sign next to the door read Effie MacDiarmid. They stood in a circle outside the room and looked at each other. Kate felt nervous.

"Well, what are you waiting for? Go on in," Kate's mom said, impatiently.

"Grammy, why don't you go in first and give Effie a heads-up that she's got more than one visitor today? We don't want to scare her," Kate said.

Her grandmother disappeared into the room. They stood in the doorway and watched, while she leaned over her sister. She touched Effie's shoulder and lightly shook her.

"Effie, are you awake?" she asked. The room was partially dark, with a bit of light coming through the curtains.

The woman lying in the hospital bed slowly opened her eyes and looked at her sister. "Winnie, what are you doing here? You were just here. Is it Saturday already?"

"No, Eff, it's Sunday."

"I can't keep track anymore. The days all seem to run together. Why are you here early? Did someone die?"

"I can't keep track either. No one has died. I've brought some visitors with me today." She turned toward the door. "You feel up to it?"

Effie pushed herself up in the bed and tried to look around her sister. "Who is it?"

"My son Ian and his wife, Maggie. Do you remember them?"

Effie smiled and said, "Yes. I remember them. I was at the wedding for Pete's sake. My brain isn't that dead, yet. Do I need to brush my hair?"

"No, Eff, you look fine. I also brought their daughter Kate and a friend of hers." Grammy motioned for them to come in.

The four slowly made their way in. Kate's mom walked to the window and pulled the drapes open. Sunlight spilled into the room. She turned and smiled at the older women.

"I'm afraid I'm probably not too presentable. I haven't quite gotten up yet..." Effie stopped as she looked from Kate's mom and dad to Kate. When she saw her, Effie squinted and put her hand around her neck. "Lizzie, is that you?" she whispered.

Grammy looked at Kate and huffed. "And she says her brain isn't addled."

"Hi, Aunt Effie," Kate said, as she approached the bed. She walked around the other side and sat on the edge.

Effie watched Kate as she sat and then looked away. Then she saw Bill and her eyes opened wide. "You brought Connor with you." She turned back to Kate. "Have you come to forgive me?"

Kate's mom sighed heavily and picked up a magazine from the table by the window and her dad leaned against the wall.

Kate looked at Bill and he moved around to her side of the bed and stood behind her. "Forgive you for what?" Kate asked and took Effie's hand.

"For what I did to you. I was so jealous and rotten to both of you. I should never have tried to start that fire. It was wrong of me, but I saw who did it. I tried to tell the sheriff and Father, but he was so mad at me," Effie whispered to Kate.

Grammy made her way to a chair in the corner and sat. Tears welled in her eyes. Kate's dad walked over to her side and put his hand on her shoulder. She looked up at him and said, "I never thought I'd hear her admit it."

"I've hated myself ever since. I've prayed to the Lord for forgiveness and I always knew he'd answer me. He has answered, because here you are. You were so beautiful at the wedding. I shouldn't have done it, but the Lord put me there for a reason. I saw him, but no one would believe me."

Kate looked up at Bill and smiled. For some reason that she couldn't explain in words she felt suddenly calm. She looked back at her great-aunt. "Effie, that was a very long time ago. As you see, we're all right."

"Have you been happy?" Effie asked and held onto Kate's hand. "Have you been together all this time? Where did you live?"

Kate saw her mom put the magazine down and seemed to pay more attention to the conversation.

"Yes. We are happy. Tell us about that night, Eff. Who did you see in the alley?" Kate squeezed the old woman's hand.

"It was that Ben Harley. He had cans of kerosene and he poured it all over the side of the building. He even used some old wood. I tried to tell Father, but he wouldn't listen to me. They blamed me, because I did try to start a fire, but it wouldn't take. It rained earlier that week and where I tried to start it was still too wet. I'm glad it didn't start, though. I only tried to scare you, but when you died, I realized what a selfish idiot I'd been." She looked at Grammy and Kate's dad. "Can you see them, too?"

"Yes, Eff, we see them, too," Grammy said.

Kate thought for a moment, before she noticed the silence in the room. "Ben Harley asked me to marry him once. I could never have married him," she said, still thinking.

"Why is that, Lizzie?" Effie asked.

"I wasn't in love with him. He'd been a bully when we were in school together. I didn't think he had a very good heart." She looked at her great-aunt. "Effie, I knew what you felt for Connor. It was thoughtless of me to go about the wedding plans the way I did. I thought you would accept, eventually, that Connor loved me. I was very insensitive and I hope you can forgive me."

"Oh, Lizzie, you're being silly. I have nothing to forgive you for. It was your day and you deserved every chance to be happy." The old woman looked up at Bill. "Mr. O'Leary, I have to warn you. Keeping up with Lizzie will be a challenge for you. She can be very determined."

Bill smiled. "I'm realizing that more every day, Effie."

"Did Winnie tell you that Delia passed away?"

"Yes, I went to the funeral in West Seattle. She's with Mother and Father now," Kate said.

"I'll be there soon, too. At least now I know that someone believes me. I'm sure our father is turning over in his grave. I hope he feels guilty for not having faith in me," Effie snickered.

"Effie, now, that's no way to think. I'm sure when you meet up with Father again he will apologize all over the place for not believing you." Kate felt suddenly uncomfortable. She had fallen into this too easily and needed to remember she was not Lizzie. "I'm going to let you visit with Winnie for a while. We need to get back home." She stood up and found Bill right behind her.

He moved around Kate, leaned over Effie and kissed her forehead. "Thank you, Miss MacDiarmid. Thanks for your help in putting a couple of pieces into a very confusing puzzle."

Effie blushed. "You're welcome, Connor. Lizzie, please come to see me, again, sometime."

"I will, Eff." She walked out of the room with Bill following. In the hallway, she leaned against the wall and looked up at him. "Ben Harley. It somehow seems right that he set the fire, but I'm missing something and I can't figure it out."

"Is it something about Ben?" Bill asked.

"Before you moved to Seattle, we attended a couple of dances together. He tried to kiss me one evening." She looked up at him. "He was a terrible kisser."

"He obviously had feelings for you, since he asked you to marry him."

"He asked Father for permission. Father agreed to the proposal, but when I laughed about it and told him I could never marry Ben, he withdrew his permission." She shook her head. "I'm still missing it. I feel it stronger than ever, but just can't remember."

Kate's mom walked out of the room and looked at her daughter. "Kate..."

"Mom, don't start."

"I'm not going to start, sweetheart," her mother said. "I'm not sure I understand any of this. I've never been a firm believer in the other-worldly stuff, but, just now, the look on Effie's face...I do believe you gave her peace."

"I never would have believed it, if I hadn't heard it with my own ears. Mom, that's the nicest thing you've said to me in ages." Kate shook her head.

"Kate, I know I can be a little hard-headed sometimes, but so can you. Just try to be patient with me. I have a lot to learn about reincarnation."

Kate's dad came out of the room. "Mom's going to catch the train back down to Seattle and will call me when she's at the station. We don't have to wait. Do you two have time for lunch?" he asked Kate and Bill.

"Sorry, but I do have some class prep for tomorrow. We also need to get geared up for round two of the hypnosis," Bill said, and looked at his watch. "Can we take a rain check?"

"That's fine," her dad said, and put his arm around her mom. "Are you two sure the hypnosis is safe? I'd rather have you speaking English and not squawking like ducks or something."

Kate stood straighter. "We came out of it okay the first time and I was really nervous then. This will be a piece of cake." She smiled up at Bill and crossed her eyes. "I'll call you later, and fill you in." She took his hand and started toward the front of the building.

When they got to the car, Bill started to laugh. "Piece of cake, huh? We're not squawking, but speaking from two different people's mouths. Are you really not nervous?"

"Okay, so I just lied to my parents. Yes, I'm nervous and that's why you're driving," she said, and handed him the keys. She walked around the car to the passenger side. "And, I'm sorry, but you don't think I'm going to tell them about our naked, midnight waltz under the crescent moon, do you?"

"Kate, sweetheart, are you okay?" Bill put the key in the door and unlocked it. He looked over the VW at her.

"Yes, no ... I don't know. Who are we?" She folded her arms on top of the car and leaned on them.

Bill dropped the keys on the seat and walked around the car. He put a hand on her shoulder and put his head against hers. "Tell me what's going on."

She shook her head and bit her lip. "I was really uncomfortable in that room, just now. I feel like I've deceived Aunt Effie. She thinks Lizzie and Connor came to visit her."

Bill leaned against the car. "In a way they did, they were there. When we were in the hallway talking, we were them. Am I making any sense at all?"

"Yes, strangely enough, you are making sense. I guess I need to accept the fact that she's a part of me. It just seems really weird."

"If it's any comfort at all, I feel the same way. Except for one thing."

Kate looked up at him. "What?"

"I can't agree with Connor, because I actually love you in slacks. You have a great butt." He smiled and started back around the car.

"Really, you like my behind?" She laughed and sat on the seat.

"Love it. There was a moment last night when you were bent over a box. Oh momma, did you look nice," he said and leaned over to kiss her.

"You do say the sweetest things, Mr. Leary."

Chapter Twenty-Eight

Bill drove them back to Kate's and she packed up a few things to take over to his house. They were going to stay there for the rest of Sunday. She didn't want to go to the grocery store and there was food at his house. He prepped for his class while she pilfered his cupboards and began a beef stew for their dinner. She planned to make biscuits, but when she'd asked him about flour and baking powder he'd given her a blank look. He had bread and a bag of noodles, she figured either would work out fine.

After dinner, they sat on the couch and watched a movie. At one point, Bill put the film on Pause and asked if she wanted to discuss their appointment for the next day. She didn't think they needed to say anything. It would be as it would be.

Kate was relieved when they stayed in bed all night and didn't go on a naked stroll. She told him so at breakfast and he laughed, but agreed.

After Bill taught his ten o'clock class, they left for Everett.

***

It took her and Bill an hour to get to Everett. They spent the better part of forty-five minutes explaining to Jeff and Anna what happened the past week. Bill said he felt as though a disconnect button was hit and his brain went in too many directions and Kate agreed with him. Then she asked if it would be possible to speak directly to Lizzie and Connor. The parapsychologists looked at each other and said they could try.

The hypnosis session started with Kate. She felt so ready; it didn't take long for her to fall into the waking sleep.

"Okay, Kate, we're going back now to the night of the fire. Feel yourself slowly move back. The time flows by gently and easily. You are safe and nothing can hurt you. Elizabeth stands by the window, looks outside and she sees someone in the alley. Kate, can you tell me what you see? Can you describe it?" Anna asked.

"It's a dirt road between the Broadview Inn and a building next door. There are trash cylinders and I can see a cat. It's hunting something. I see a shadow over by one of the cylinders. It's dark in the alley, so I'm not sure what I'm seeing. Now he's moving one of the bins. It has wood in it and he's tipping it over by the wall of the Inn. He's picking up a tin container and pouring something on the wood. Before he disappeared he looked up at the window where I'm standing...oh." Kate started to laugh.

"What's happening, Kate?"

"Connor has put his hands around my waist and is kissing my neck."

"Can you still see the man in the alley?"

"No, Connor has distracted me and pulls the curtains closed. I think I know the man in the alley, but I can't focus. Connor's hands..." Kate giggled.

"Kate, if you had to make a guess who the man is, can you come up with a name?"

"I thought it might be Ben Harley, but it was dark and it didn't make sense."

"Why didn't it make sense?"

"Why would he be moving a trash bin down in the alley? He worked at the bank, it makes no sense."

"Is it possible you saw Ben Harley preparing to start the fire?"

"It's possible, I suppose. Effie told Bill and Kate she couldn't get her fire to stay lit. Eff said she saw Ben Harley in the alley."

"Do you think Effie started the fire?"

"No, I believed her when she said it couldn't have been hers. I wonder if it's possible he's still here. I think it's possible he's here." Kate felt confused as to why she would think it was Ben, but the feeling was strong.

"What do you mean, Kate? Who is still here?"

"Like Connor and me. Is it possible the man in the alley is still here, too?" Kate said quietly.

"Kate, would it be possible for us to speak to Lizzie?"

Kate's eyebrows creased. "You are speaking to Lizzie. You have been this whole time."

"Okay, Kate, we're going to come back to the present time. When you awaken you will feel calm and refreshed, ten, nine, eight, seven, six you're starting to become alert and your eyes are opening. Five, four, three, two, one, now, you're awake and relaxed." Anna sat up in her chair. "How do you feel, Kate?"

She opened her eyes and looked at Bill. She tightened her grip on his and said, "Babe, I think there may be someone else having dreams."

"You could be right. I wonder if it was the person who watched your apartment the night before last." He helped her sit up.

Jeff sat in a chair across from them. "If this is the case and there are three of you with progressive dreams from the same place and time, it would be unprecedented and amazing."

"And a bit creepy," Kate said, and leaned against Bill. "I don't have a clue how to find him."

"I think we can safely say he's been watching my house. Do you ever remember seeing anyone at your old address or your parents' house?"

"No, not that I can think of," Kate answered. "I don't understand any of this. The one thing I really want to know, is how do we let it go?"

"It seems Lizzie and Connor want their murder solved," Anna said. "Maybe once the shadow man is identified, they'll be able to rest in peace."

Kate shook her head. "I wish I could think of someone who looked like Ben, but there's no one."

Bill went under hypnosis, but hadn't seen the man in the alley. When Anna and Jeff asked to speak to Connor, they were given the same answer that they'd gotten from Kate.

Anna and Jeff gave them some advice and techniques on how to control their thoughts when Lizzie and Connor seemed to be taking over. They discussed meditation and breathing exercises. It helped calm Kate down and feel more centered.

Chapter Twenty-nine

Bill drove back to his house. They were quiet and he thought about the latest discovery and what it could mean to them. As he pulled off the freeway and turned onto the road to Highwood, Kate undid her seatbelt and scooted over the seat next to him.

"Darling woman, you know riding in a car without a seatbelt on is against the law," he said.

"I know, I just didn't like being so far away from you, and we're almost there. As long as you don't run any stop signs or red lights, we should be all right." She leaned against him, and put her hand on his leg.

"Miss Sullivan, are we going to have to discuss appropriate places for touching excitable parts of the body? I already want to pull the truck over and take you, right here, out in public," he said, and smiled.

She moved her hand. "I'll behave, sweetheart. I guess this would be a good time to tell you my hand has developed a mind of its own and does go wherever it wants."

"I'll remember that." He stopped at a red light and put his arm around her.

He drove the rest of the way in silence and let his mind think about her body for a change. When Bill pulled into his driveway behind Kate's VW, he heard her whisper, *manly truck* and had to smile. He got out of the cab, walked around to the passenger side and opened her door.

Kate looked out the front window at her car. "Bill, does my car usually sit so low?"

He looked through the door window and realized there was something wrong with the car.

"Stay here, babe," he said, and moved to the front of the truck. He looked at each of the tires on the car and then walked back to her. He took his cell phone out of his pocket. "It looks like they were slashed, probably with a knife or box cutter. I'm going to call the police." He helped her down out of the truck and gave her a hug. "I don't understand it. This kind of stuff doesn't happen up here." He saw her looking at the house, not her car. "What is it?"

She turned him around and pointed to the front door. "You didn't leave the door open, did you?"

"Dammit, honey, stay here. I'll be right back."

"No," she said, and grabbed his arm. "I don't want to stand here alone. Call the cops and when they arrive we'll go in with them. If someone is still in the house, I don't want you to get hurt."

"But ..."

"Please, Bill, no buts. Just call the police."

***

The police came and checked inside the house. Once they were sure it was safe they allowed Kate and Bill to enter.

They all stopped and stood in the doorway. Kate's mouth dropped open and she sucked in her breath. She put her hand over her mouth, not sure if she might scream. Bill took her other hand and put his arm around her shoulders.

On the wall, in the entryway, the word **WHORE** had been scrawled in big, black letters. When they looked into the living room, it didn't seem there was a part of the room that hadn't been destroyed. More foul words were written everywhere she looked. The painting he had hung above the fire place was pulled down and shredded, as were parts of the couch and recliner. She felt glad she had taken the wedding dress back to her parents' house, but wasn't glad about all the destruction.

"Oh, Bill, I'm so sorry. This is terrible," she whispered.

229

They continued through the rest of the house. In the kitchen, they found every plate, glass and coffee mug broken. The blinds hung sideways on the windows and it looked as though parts of the stove had been dismantled. The burners lay on the floor, surrounded by shards of glass. A couple of the doors on the cupboards were pulled off. In the bedroom, Bill's queen-size bed was shredded and stuffing and springs were everywhere around it. His nightstand was turned over; the clock and lamp smashed.

When they walked back into the living room, Kate looked at one of the policemen. "Officer, I think I know who did all of this. My ex-boyfriend hasn't been dealing with our break up very well. It could have been him."

"What makes you think that, Miss Sullivan?" the officer asked.

"He was pretty aggressive with me last week. I was packing up my things at the place we shared and, well, he's gotten abusive. My mom and dad have seen it happen. I could be wrong, but ..." She looked up at Bill. "I'm so sorry."

Bill hugged her again. "There's nothing for you to be sorry about, sweetheart. Nothing."

"What's your ex-boyfriends name?"

"Henry Parsons."

***

Bill called his insurance agent, who arrived at the house within an hour. He took pictures of everything and wrote down notes. Bill packed a bag and found his class folder. He collected Kate's case and put them both into his truck.

Kate found a broom in the kitchen and swept up the pieces of glass and plates. She realized the garbage can under the sink wouldn't be big enough to hold the debris. She went out to Bill's garage and found a bigger bin and dragged it into the kitchen.

In her head, Kate felt certain Henry was the one who'd done this. It made her so angry with him and the only thing that would let him off the hook would be a great alibi. Who else would write such terrible things on the wall?

When Bill finished with the police, he joined her in the kitchen. Kate looked out the sliding door at Bill's backyard. He put his hands around her waist and kissed her neck.

"Darling man, I'm so sorry this happened," she said, again.

"Kate, don't blame yourself. You couldn't have known Henry would react this way."

"I still have some time before I go back to work. I can help you get the walls cleaned up; I guess get everything cleaned up." She sighed.

"Cleaning won't do it with the walls. They'll have to be primed before they're re-painted. He used a black marker, according to the police," Bill said. "I was thinking about painting them, so now I have the incentive to do the job."

"Mr. Leary, do you have a minute?" the insurance agent asked from the kitchen doorway.

Bill went over the findings and amounts. The agent said they'd get a check to him by the end of the week, so he could begin repairs. There was something mentioned about possible legal issues if the perpetrator was found and charges files, but they could go over all that later. As the agent left, he asked Bill if he had a place to stay. The insurance company would be happy to arrange for a hotel room.

"He has a place to stay," Kate said, and turned from the window. "Let me give you the address and landline number, just in case Bill's cell phone is turned off."

Bill locked up the house and drove them over to Kate's apartment in his truck.

"The agent said they're including money to buy you a new set of tires. Since it was part of the destruction, they're willing to include it in my homeowners insurance," Bill said as he drove the three blocks and pulled into the driveway. He turned off the engine.

"I'll have to let the landlord know you'll be staying for a while," Kate said.

They sat silently in the truck. Kate wanted to go back to his house and continue getting things cleaned up.

"Sweetheart, are you getting hungry?" Bill asked, and kissed her hand.

"I didn't even think about that. I haven't gotten to the grocery store yet," she said.

Bill put his fingers on her lips. "No worries. Let's get cleaned up, dump off the bags and we'll go out to eat. We can stop at the grocery store on our way back."

Kate kissed his fingers. "My hero," she said and smiled.

He leaned over, put his lips on hers and lightly flicked them with his tongue. "I love you, Miss Sullivan."

She took in a breath. "I love you, too, Mr. Leary."

He straightened up. "Now, if you start that flirty thing, I doubt we'll get any food," he said as he opened his door. "And I'm really hungry."

"Me, flirty? You were the one doing the touchy, tongue thing." She laughed and opened hers.

Bill got out of the truck and grinned. He pulled the bags from behind the seat, and slammed the door shut. She watched him walk around to her side, look up at her and then freeze. She saw something that looked hard and cold pressed behind his ear.

"Move away from the door, asshole," a voice growled.

Bill looked up at her. She had turned in the seat and could see Henry press a gun to the side of Bill's head. She briefly thought *this week just won't give up*. She stepped down out of the truck as Henry grabbed Bill's collar and pulled him back.

"For the love of God, Henry, have you lost your mind completely?" Kate asked, angrily.

"Shut up, slut. I'm not the one getting hurt today. This fuck, who turned you into a whore, is getting his brains blown out." Henry stared at the back of Bill's head, and grinned manically. "We were doing just fine until he came along. You would have married me, eventually."

"No Henry, things weren't fine. Remember the accident when my hip was dislocated? Do you remember how little we talked?" She moved to the middle of the driveway and tried to turn his attention away from Bill.

Henry followed her with his eyes and the gun. When she stopped, he pushed Bill forward and pointed the gun at Kate. "Why are you being such a bitch? You love me and you know it, Lizzie. You should never have married him. It should have been me, but no, you had to laugh me off and tell your father you wouldn't marry if you weren't in love. You know it was only my love that could have kept you alive. You weren't supposed to die in the fire anyway. Just the iron-smith, Connor. He was supposed to save you, then die."

Kate stared at him, and listened carefully to all the words that came out of his mouth. "*Laughing at you*. That was it. That was the thing I couldn't remember." She shook her head. "Ben?"

"I couldn't believe you never knew it was me. I supported you all these years. I waited patiently for you to come around and marry me. I found you at Gonzaga and I followed you here. It should have been me, Lizzie, not this fucking asshole. You laughed at me. How could you?" Henry shouted at her.

"Henry, you look nothing like Ben. How was I supposed to know it was you? I'll never marry you. Not in this life, not in the next one. Get that through your thick skull. I don't love you, I'm not sure I ever did?" she shouted back.

"You asked me to marry you when I turned sixteen. I wasn't adult enough to know what to say or how to act. What did you expect? I was too young."

"You bitch..." Henry began, but Bill plowed into him, grabbed his wrist and pointed the gun skyward.

A shot went off and caused Kate to jump. She watched as the two men danced around the driveway, both trying to get control of each other and the gun. Henry's hand was under Bills jaw and he tried to push Bill away. She could see the muscle in Bill's arm flex as the gun shifted around.

She watched as Bill fought to get the gun out of the mad man's grip and hit Henry in the stomach.

Kate heard sirens in the distance and hoped the landlady or someone in the neighborhood called the police. Another loud bang went off again and something hit her in the stomach. She put her hands just above her pants and felt something warm run through her fingers. She brought her hand up and saw blood. She swallowed and fell to her knees. She looked up and saw the two men frozen, as they stared at her.

Bill pulled his arm back and punched Henry so hard a couple of teeth flew out of his mouth. Henry fell backwards, sat on the driveway pavement and fell flat on his back. He held his mouth and moaned.

Bill knelt down in front of Kate. He'd pulled out his cell phone and dialed 9-1-1 for the second time that day. Kate sat back on her heels and stared into his eyes.

"No, no, no, not again. We can't be separated again," she whispered. She put her hand on his chest and grabbed a handful of his shirt. "Tell me this didn't happen. Tell me everything is going to be fine."

Bill wrapped his arms around her and talked into the phone. She heard him give the address and tell the dispatcher what happened.

***

Bill looked up as a squad car pulled into the driveway and the officers who'd been to his house earlier, got out of the cruiser.

One of the officers helped Bill with Kate and called for the medics. The other policeman, scooped up Henry's gun. He patted him down and cuffed his hands behind his back.

"He broke my fucking jaw. I want him arrested for assault!" Henry shouted, as blood ran out of his mouth. "He's a menace to society and stole my woman."

Bill refused to pay any attention to what Henry yelled. Kate's head rested on his thigh and his hand pressed on the wound in her stomach. He tried to keep her calm while blood ran through his fingers.

Kate kept saying, "Not again, not again," and cried. He kept thinking back to the night of the fire, when he and Lizzie fell through the stairs. It couldn't happen again. Maybe they weren't destined to be together and God was trying to get his message across to them, but he couldn't even comprehend that line of thought. Kate looked up at him and tried to say something. He spoke to one of the officers and put his hand behind her head. He couldn't hear what she said because a voice in his head made too much noise. He saw her grimace and sat down behind her.

"Bill?" she whispered. He leaned over closer to her. "There's a pain stabbing my stomach and my legs have gone numb."

He looked down at her and saw her beautiful blue eyes tear up. He felt his throat tighten and choked, "Sweetheart, I'm right here. The ambulance is on the way. I know it must hurt, but everything will be fine. Help is on the way."

"I love you so much. I want us together, but what if destiny says no? What if we can't be with each other?"

235

"Kate, I thought that, too. I don't think that's right. Why would God bring us back together only to split us up again? I've decided not to think about destiny anymore. We're together and always will be. I'm not going to lose you again. You'd better listen to me, because I love you and you own me. We're not giving up," he said in her ear.

He looked down at her again and saw her eyes cross and close. "Kate, wake up. Stay with me, my lass." Bill looked up at the sky and held Kate in his arms. "Whoever you are don't do this again. We're innocent in all this mess. Please, don't take her from me!" he shouted at the sky. He felt tears roll down his checks and watched her closely to make sure she was still breathing.

Chapter Thirty

Kate saw a bright, warm light. Voices came from it, called to her and drew her near. She held back. She didn't want to go there. She thought she knew what it meant and she didn't feel ready to give up. It wasn't her time. She wanted to stay where she was and not let go. Footfalls sounded in her ears and pounded like a drum or heart beat. Something moved in the light. It became a shadow and walked toward her. Kate's eyes cleared enough that she could tell it was a woman and a man. They walked hand in hand. She took a step back when she realized it was Lizzie and Connor.

They walked right up to her as though it were a sunny day. Lizzie wore the white wedding dress with her hair piled on top of her head. She looked so beautiful. Connor wore his dark suit and looked so much like Bill, Kate wanted to reach out and touch him.

"Am I dead?" Kate asked.

"No, dear, you're fighting for your life and that's good. We want you to continue," Lizzie said. She looked up at Connor and smiled.

"We came here to thank you for holding our story dear and close to your heart," Connor said, with his Irish accent. "We want you to know how very grateful we are that you and Bill allowed us to invade your lives all these years. You let us see each other again and that is a great gift."

"Wait, you've been apart all these years?"

"Aye, that we have. When you and Bill came together we were allowed to be together again. Now that the puzzle is solved, we can retire quietly."

"What do you mean the puzzle is solved? I'm confused," Kate asked.

"We now know who set the fire. Ben confessed it to you. He'll be dealt with properly when his time comes," Lizzie said and continued to smile. "You have to go back, Kate. You have a life to build now and I think there will be nothing but joy for you and Bill. I believe he loves you so very much, that you could ask him for the moon and he would find a way to give it to you. Thank you for your help, dear Kate." Lizzie reached out her hand.

"Wait. Have you haunted us all these years or what? How did we know your story?" Kate asked and reached toward Lizzie. When she tried to touch the outstretched hand, hers just went through it.

"We gave you our memories. You were open to them. We didn't know that they would affect you and Bill so, but we knew you would be able to sort them out and discover the truth." Lizzie looked up at Connor. "We want to give you a gift."

"We know you'll carry our love with you always. We are grateful beyond words to you and Bill. Please, enjoy our gift."

"What gift?" Kate asked and felt her hair blow around her face as a gentle, warm breeze caressed her face. She closed her eyes briefly and when she opened them she stood on a dirt road. The air around her was cool and the sun peaked over a ridge.

As she looked down the road, she saw green fields along both sides. They stretched on for what seemed like miles and miles. There were also gray stone walls that fenced off the fields from the roads. They were made of flat slate stones, piled one on top of another, neatly packed with grass growing between them. It was charming.

A hand reached around her and patted her stomach. When she looked down at herself, she found she had gained a few pounds and gotten very big.

"Are you ready to head back?" a familiar voice asked.

Kate looked over her shoulder and saw Bill behind her. "Back to where?"

"To the hotel. We need to get some breakfast, before we continue the search for Connor's home. You are feeding my son in there and we have to keep him strong." Bill smiled.

She put her hands on her stomach and felt something move. She turned around and put her hands on Bills cheeks. "Dear man, I love you. I just want to make sure you know that."

"I love you, too, sweetheart. We've only got a couple more weeks before Connor William makes an appearance. I don't want to waste a single moment." He took her hand, kissed the palm and they began to walk along the road.

When they came to a cross road, she saw a sign that read, "Dublin" with an arrow pointed in that direction. She realized they were in Ireland and she began to hear voices and a noise beeped in her ear.

The atmosphere around her felt heavy and she found it difficult to breathe. She closed her eyes, and tried to calm herself, but when she wanted to open her eyes again, she couldn't. They felt taped shut.

She finally got them open a little. They wouldn't focus and she couldn't tell where she was, but it seemed familiar. After a few minutes, it became clear she was back in the hospital. She wondered if she'd given birth to the baby. She tried to move, but her stomach screamed in pain and she decided it was best to remain still. She found she could move her head though and tried to look around. There was something brown just to her right and as her eyes cleared she could tell it was a head of hair. She saw Bill's blue eyes squint at her. She touched his cheek and tried to smile.

"Hi," she whispered. She saw the blue eyes fill and he stood up. He leaned over, and kissed her eyes, cheeks, nose and finished with her lips. "You have coffee breath, babe." She smiled.

"Sorry," he whispered, butted his forehead on her chin and let out a sigh.

She moved her hand trough his hair. "Hey, it's okay. I love coffee breath."

"I don't think I've ever been so scared in my life, Kate."

"Now I'm sorry. I wasn't awake to comfort you."

"The fact that you're speaking," he lifted his head to look into her eyes. "It's all I could ever ask for, babe. I love you so much."

"I know you do."

"How do you know that?"

"It was simple to work out. Every time I went into my weird Lizzie mode, you only called for me to come back. You didn't call for Lizzie. I knew then and I know it now."

"Oh, my God, you're awake!!!" She heard a woman shout and something went plop by the door.

Kate turned her head and saw her mom walk toward her. Kate's dad appeared at the end of the bed.

Her mom grabbed her other hand and held it to her heart. "Thank God, how are you feeling, baby?"

"Not real alert yet, Mom," Kate said, and tried to keep her eyes open. Her dad came up next to her mom and put his hand around her wrist. "Hi, Daddy."

"Sweetheart, I don't want this to happen anymore. My blood pressure won't take it." He kissed her hand.

"Me, too." Kate's eyes closed.

"Maybe we should let her rest," she heard her mom say.

"No, I can stay awake for a few minutes. Did I have the baby?" She looked at Bill. She saw his brows come together and was suddenly scared. "I didn't lose the baby, did I?"

Bill looked up at her parents'. They all seemed tongue tied. "Sweetheart, as far as I know you weren't pregnant. You were shot by Henry. Do you remember what happened?" Bill asked.

"Oh, I see, I think," she said. She started to laugh quietly. "I had the most amazing dream."

The room went silent and she looked at her three loved ones who stood around the bed. She saw her mom and dad exchange glances.

"No, really it was a great dream." She looked up at Bill. "I saw Lizzie and Connor and they thanked us for getting the puzzle solved. They said the one that murdered them would have a lot to answer for in time." She realized slowly, that her parents could never understand the importance of dreams. "Okay, you two need to go home and get some rest. I need to talk to Bill."

Her parents' looked at Bill on the other side of the bed.

"What time is it, anyway?"

"4:15 in the morning," her dad said.

"Yeah, you need sleep, but tell the nurse about the coffee you dropped, Mom."

"How did you know?"

"I can smell it," Kate said, and pulled her mom down to kiss her cheek. "I love you, Mom. I love you, too, Dad. Come back later, when you've gotten some rest."

"Sweetheart, I like your young man very much. We'll talk later," her mom whispered in her ear. "Okay, come on Ian. They need to talk." She pulled Kate's dad to the door, then turned back and looked at Bill. "Be sure to let her get some rest, Bill."

"I will, Maggie." Bill sat back down and looked at Kate. "Your mother is very interesting. I think after we got the police settled down, and the surgeon gave us a good report on the bullet wound, she had my life story in about five minutes. I could be wrong, but I think she likes me."

"She just said as much. That's my mom." Kate smiled, and closed her eyes again. "If nothing else, she's consistent."

"After we visited Effie, your mom went online trying to find books on reincarnation and 'other worldly things', as she likes to say," he continued.

"Oh dear, we may have created a monster. I'll keep her at bay."

"So tell the truth, where does it hurt?" Bill asked, and put her hand on his cheek and held it there.

"My stomach feels like I've had someone with spikes run through it."

"Not those horrendous spikes?" Bill said and chuckled. "The surgeon said the bullet managed not to hit anything important. You have some stitches, but he said everything should be just fine."

"Yeah, the damn bullet from Henry's gun. What happened with him anyway?"

"I broke his jaw," Bill said a bit sheepishly. "I didn't mean to, but sort of meant to."

"Don't feel guilty, babe. Remember I kicked him in the balls. He deserved worse."

"The police listened to both sides of the story. Henry started to act weird and said things about how I'd stolen his woman and he felt fine. He wanted the cuffs off and his gun back. When the police said no, he went a little berserk and they arrested him. He may be charged with attempted murder, and will be charged with carrying a concealed weapon. That's a federal offense, you know? They said as soon as you woke up, they want to talk to you, but only when you're ready. If you want to press charges, he could be put away for a very long time. Otherwise, it could be settled as some sort of mischief." Bill smiled. "They said I could be there when they question you, to give you support and all that manly stuff."

Kate laughed. "Ow, ow...don't make me laugh, it hurts. I do like the support you give," she said as her eyes started to close.

"Hey, before you go to sleep again, what was the rest of the amazing dream?"

Kate's closed her eyes, but she smiled. "Oh right, it was you and me." She opened her eyes and drank him in. "You and me, not Lizzie and Connor, but they were there. They gave me a gift and it's one I'll treasure for a really long time. After they left, you and I walked along a road in Ireland. We were searching for Connor's home in Cork and I was pregnant."

"Pregnant? I guess that's where the baby came in. Were we married?" Bill asked.

"I'm not sure."

"I want to, you know, as soon as you're able and willing."

"Good, I want that, too. I may have to move into your house. I hope the new landlord will understand."

"Oh yeah, babe, I do have some bad news. After the police arrived and arrested Henry, your landlord came out of the upstairs part of the house. She said she couldn't have this kind of stuff happen around her house and you'd have to move."

"Crap," Kate said and frowned.

"So your dad and I are going to get the truck again. I've got a couple of students I'm sure will want to earn some extra credits and we'll have you all moved into my house before you get out of here."

She smiled and opened her eyes. "See, you are being supportive. I love that about you, although I think you're a bit sneaky, too."

"I have no idea what you're talking about," he said and looked hurt with pouty lips. "So, you were pregnant. Did we know if it was a boy or girl?

"It was a boy. We're going to name him Connor William. We watched the sunrise and looked at the walls," she said as she drifted back to sleep.

***

That afternoon, Maggie told Bill to go home and get cleaned up. She didn't come right out and say it, but he knew he needed a shower. He got a taxi back to Kate's apartment to pick up his truck and then drove back to his house. It was still a mess, but he was able to get himself cleaned up and shaved.

He left the hospital at four o'clock in the afternoon and was back by eight in the evening. He walked into Kate's room and carried an armload of flowers in a vase. He found her sitting up in bed, sipping water through a straw. Her cheeks had color in them and she was a little more alert than the morning before.

"Oh, darling man, did you clean out your garden?" Kate asked as she smelled the flowers.

"No, these are from that wonderful nursery called Safeway. They have everything a manly man could possibly need." He smiled and gave her a quick kiss, in front of her mom and everything.

Kate's dad walked in behind Bill and smiled. Bill moved the flowers to the nightstand, while Ian walked up to his daughter and took her hand.

"Mr. Leary and I have just had quite a talk," her dad said.

Bill straightened up and smiled at her. "Indeed we did."

Maggie stood up next to her husband. "What have you two been talking about?" she asked.

Ian grinned. "Bill here needs to borrow our van, sweetheart."

"I thought you were going to get the big truck again to move my stuff," Kate said.

"No, my dear, I have to get a new bed. Henry shredded my old one; I have to get a new mattress and box spring." Bill continued to smile.

"But you have your manly truck, babe. Why would you need the van?"

Bill just continued to smile at her. "Since it's started to rain I think the van will help keep it from getting wet."

"So what does the van have to do with this serious talk you two just had?" Kate asked and looked from Bill to her dad.

"He also asked my permission to marry you, my daughter," her dad said. He looked at his wife. "Sorry, I didn't talk to you first, Maggie. It was spur of the moment and one of those manly things." Ian started to laugh and blushed.

"So, what was your answer, Dad?"

"He said yes and gave us his blessing," Bill said. He wiggled his pinkie around where he thought Kate would notice and she finally saw the ring. She looked up at him.

Bill grinned at her, again. "So, will you? Marry me, that is?" He put his chin in the palm of his hand and winked at her.

He'd found the box with the beautiful engagement ring that belonged to Lizzie on the floor of his living room. He took it off his pinkie and slipped it onto her finger. She pulled him down to her and kissed him. He looked into her gorgeous blue eyes.

"You are so sneaky sometimes, but why do I think there is something else going on with the van?" She asked.

"No, there's nothing really with the van. We could use if for a honeymoon camping trip, maybe. I'm not sure I want to stay in a hotel."

Kate nodded. "That sounds like a very good idea."

Going to Another Place

A man, from 2008, falls 48 floors from a building in Seattle and wakes up in 1815 England. A woman, in 1815 England, watches a bright star fall from the sky. She travels to the future, but can't stay due to her lack of immunity to the 21st century diseases.

Michael Drury and Emma Wallace have fallen in love but are torn between two worlds. He has family in the 21st century. She wants to stay with him, but continues to grow very ill, very fast.

Spanning almost 200 years, will their love be able to exist in the same time?

ABOUT THE AUTHOR

Lauren Marie lives with her four cats in Western Washington State. She is the author of Going to Another Place and The Men of Haller Lake - Trilogy.

In her other existence, she is an amateur paranormal investigator. She has had many unusual experiences which have put in appearances in some of her stories, most recently in Ghost Hunt 101. She is still trying to find a way to incorporate "Buddy" the ghost dog on State Street into a story.

Although, she has been focusing her current efforts in the paranormal romance and time-travel genres, she has also written general fiction and strictly paranormal.
Visit her at laurenmariebooks.com

Made in the USA
San Bernardino, CA
01 May 2014